The Accidental Elopement

A Chance Romance

Maggie Dallen

LYRICAL PRESS
Kensington Publishing Corp.
www.kensingtonbooks.com

First Electronic Edition: November 2016
eISBN-13: 978-1-60183-469-0
eISBN-10: 1-60183-469-1

First Print Edition: November 2016
ISBN-13: 978-1-60183-470-6
ISBN-10: 1-60183-470-5

Printed in the United States of America

First comes love, then comes marriage—or is it the other way around?

Lucia is an Italian spitfire with big dreams like her billionaire grandfather. But she wants to become a top tier fashion designer, not the heir to the family business in Italy. Now is her only chance to forge her own path. And what better place to start than in New York City? But working behind a bar doesn't exactly pay the rent. Her trust fund would come in handy, but she needs to get married first. Luckily, she may have found the perfect husband candidate in her co-worker, who just happens to be the most charismatic and devastatingly gorgeous man she's ever met . . .

There's more to Ryan's charming smile than meets the eye—he's out for revenge and working for his enemy is his best bet at getting it. When Lucia comes to him with her crazy plan, he sees a perfect opportunity to make his move. But doing that could mean hurting his new wife. They say nothing's sweeter than revenge—but "they" never met a woman like Lucia . . .

THE ACCIDENTAL ELOPEMENT
A Chance Romance

Books by Maggie Dallen

The Chance Series
The Accidental Engagement
The Accidental Boyfriend
The Accidental Elopement

Published by Kensington Publishing Corporation

Chapter 1

Lucia had exactly nine dollars and thirty-six cents in her pocket as she fought her way onto the crowded F-train heading downtown. Enough to buy one more coffee and a bagel—a combo she'd come to adore during her six-week stint in New York—but not much else.

She reached through a thick crowd of people so she could hold onto the cold metal pole in the middle of the train to keep her balance. *The subway*. That was one thing she would not miss when she left. But even that bit of optimism was enough to bring tears to her eyes. Who was she kidding? She was going to miss everything about this city, even the crowded, smelly subway.

She had just enough left on her Metrocard for a train to the airport but her credit card had long since maxed out and she had no clue how she could pay for the airfare.

You could call Grandpa.

She shook her head in disgust. It was bad enough that she was going back to Italy with her tail between her legs; there was no way she would beg her grandfather for the airfare home. When her grandmother was alive, she used to describe him as overprotective. More like smothering. Of course he only had her best interests at heart—as did her ex-fiancé—but that didn't mean they knew what was best. She would be the one to pave her future, even if it meant she failed.

Lucia watched as the subway door opened and closed before continuing on downtown. The next stop was SoHo. She knew where she had to go. If she was being honest with herself, she'd known where she was heading the moment she'd walked away from her disappointing meeting with her former boss—her last lifeline to the new life she'd been working for this past month.

Stifling a heavy sigh, she shifted to make room for another passenger who needed access to the pole. An older Hispanic man who was sitting on one of the orange plastic seats made a gesture, silently asking if she'd like his seat. She forced a smile and shook her head. "No thank you, I'm getting off at the next stop."

Daniel's hotel loomed taller than any other building in the trendy downtown neighborhood. It was the closest thing to a skyscraper amidst small boutiques and brownstones. She had the address that Jack and Holly had given her when they'd tracked her down that first week after she'd impulsively hopped on the plane to the States. Her friends had found her with alarming ease and had made her promise that she would go to Daniel if she needed any help.

Daniel was one of her grandfather's business partners—but he was also a friend, she reminded herself. She was certain he knew she was in the city but he and his wife, Ivy, had given her the space she'd asked for. They'd given her room to create a new life, one that had nothing to do with her grandfather's money or expectations.

And she'd done a hell of a job. Six weeks into her "new life" and she was about to beg a family friend for money so she could run back home. Lucia paused before the glass doors of the hotel and drew in a long deep breath of the cool fall air. Maybe she should ask Jack and Holly if she could stay with them in Paris instead. But that would just be delaying the inevitable. She exhaled with a loud sigh and pulled open the heavy door.

The hotel smelled cozy and clean—like a home away from home. Which it was, she supposed, for the wealthy and famous who could afford to stay at a place like this. The lobby was quiet but the clerk behind the front desk was busy talking to guests who appeared to be checking in.

Lucia paced around the reception area. She could wait; it wasn't like she was in a rush to humiliate herself. The lobby opened into a bar area, where an empty hostess stand stood and beyond that an empty restaurant sat perfectly set up, waiting for the next crowd.

Perching on a barstool, Lucia kept an eye on the front desk. Maybe she should have called first.

"Would you like to see a bar menu?"

Lucia swiveled around to find the bartender watching her expectantly.

"We're not serving dinner yet but we have some appetizers available."

The bartender was hot. Like, movie star hot. Lucia's mouth went dry and her ability to speak English took a momentary hiatus from her brain. This guy was intimidatingly hot. Dark hair and bright blue eyes with a chiseled jaw—he should play a superhero in a movie.

When one corner of his mouth turned up in an amused smile, Lucia came back to her senses. "No, thank you. I'm not hungry." Her stomach gave a little whine of protest but she ignored it. Those nine dollars had to last her until she got home.

The bartender put away the little menu but didn't move. "Something to drink?"

Lucia shook her head. "No, thanks. I'm just here to meet someone."

The hot bartender's eyebrows lifted in new understanding. "Oh, you're here for the job?"

"Um...."

He looked down at his watch and then back to her with that amused, sexy-as-hell little smile. "You're early."

"Oh. I...." Before she could finish, he tossed the dishrag he'd been holding under the bar and headed toward the register. "But you're in luck. I'm the one conducting the interviews so we can get started whenever you're ready."

Lucia watched him dig through a stack of papers next to the register. *Interviews?*

He came back to her and set a paper and pen in front of her. "Application for Employment" was printed across the top. Lucia felt a hysterical laugh building in her lungs, threatening to escape. A job? He thought she was here for a job?

Lucia picked up the pen and toyed with it as she scanned the questions. What was she even supposed to be applying for?

"Do you have any waitressing experience?" hot guy asked.

Ah. Well, that answered that. For a moment she considered lying but then thought better of it. "Not really." She glanced up to see the bartender's reaction but he was busy wiping down the glassware.

Lucia looked over at the front desk to see if the clerk was available. She wondered if Daniel was even in the building. She had an image of him walking into the bar that he owned and finding his billionaire business partner's daughter bussing tables.

The laughter that had been threatening came out as a choking noise which caught the bartender's attention. "You all right?"

Lucia nodded as the bartender filled a glass of water and set it down in front of her. At that moment her stomach growled so loudly it would have been comical if it wasn't so mortifying.

"You sure you don't want to see that bar menu?"

Those piercing, sapphire eyes were filled with amusement as he rested his elbows on the bar, bringing his face closer to hers.

She shook her head. "No, thanks. I can't, uh...I mean, I don't have any money on me." The amusement faded and was replaced by a look of understanding that was so sweet and so welcome, it was enough to bring tears to her eyes.

"Well you're in luck because employees eat for free."

Lucia looked down at her still-blank application and then back up to the bartender. "I got the job?"

He laughed as he turned back to the register and started tapping at the screen. "Let's not get ahead of ourselves. But while you're interviewing, I think we can say you're practically staff."

He glanced at her over his shoulder. "I won't tell the big bosses if you don't."

Lucia thought of Daniel, the biggest of the big bosses at this hotel. "Your secret is safe with me."

That earned her a full-blown smile and—oh my God, the man had dimples. Full-on dimples, along with a cleft in his chin—it was the kind of smile one found on the underwear models gracing the billboards in Times Square, not your neighborhood bartender.

And that smile was focused on her. It was too much—like staring directly into the sun. Lucia dropped her head and pretended to study the blank application in front of her. The only sound around them was a busboy cleaning silverware at the far end of the bar and the distant sound of the front desk clerk dealing with the same guests who'd been hogging his attention since Lucia had arrived.

She heard the bartender moving toward her and started filling in the easy blanks. Her first name, her age....the last name she left blank. What was she doing? Her grandfather would have a fit if he found out she was applying to be a waitress.

But Grandpa isn't here.

That thought brought with it a now-familiar heady feeling of freedom. It was that terrifyingly exciting sense of leaping into the unknown that had gotten her through the past six weeks on her own in a foreign country. She'd paved her own way quite successfully for a little while there. Her friends in the fashion industry had set her up with an internship with Eleanor Fallone, one of the biggest up-and-comers in the business. Lucia had thrived in the fast-paced lifestyle and some fashion bloggers and buyers had even started to take an interest in some of her designs.

But then Eleanor had announced that she and her team were heading to London for the next show and there was no room on the team for an intern who couldn't pay her own way.

And while the internship had been an incredible learning experience, it was definitely not lucrative. She'd blown through the little savings she'd tucked away so until she could gain access to her trust fund…well, she was at her grandfather's mercy. A fact she just knew he was counting on. The trust her mother had set up before she died stipulated that she didn't get access to the money until she turned thirty…or until she married. *Please.* As if a ring on the finger meant instant financial responsibility. Or maybe her mother had fallen victim to the chauvinistic idea that men were better with money. She didn't remember her mother but that didn't sound like her. She was willing to bet her entire trust fund that her old-fashioned grandfather had inserted the marriage exception. Not that he was that chauvinistic—he was just that romantic. He'd had the perfect marriage and the perfect family and it was completely beyond him that not everyone lived and died for love.

"Hey, are you all right?"

Lucia's head shot up and she found the bartender watching her, the brilliant smile replaced by a frown of concern. Lucia glanced down to see that she was gripping the pen like a sword and she was dangerously close to tears for the fifth time that day. Drawing a deep breath, she forced a smile.

"I'm fine," she said. She loosened her death grip on the pen and gestured toward the application. "Just not sure this is the best idea…."

He leaned back against an ice bin and crossed his arms. "Do you need a job?"

Lucia fingered the nine dollars and thirty-six cents through her jeans pocket. "Desperately."

The corner of his lips twitched in amusement at her pathetic sigh. "So what's the problem?"

Lucia stared at him, her mouth open and ready to speak but no words came out. Was she actually considering doing this? Could she really get a job like any normal person her age? She could make her own money and stay in New York. Maybe she could even apply to the Fashion Institute like Eleanor had suggested.

Heart racing with excitement, Lucia's eye was caught by the blank spaces that she couldn't fill in. "I, uh…I don't have any experience."

The sympathetic look in his eyes was so sweet she thought she might melt. "Are you willing to learn?"

Lucia nodded with a little too much enthusiasm. "Absolutely."

He rewarded her with another swoon-worthy smile. "That's all I need to hear."

Lucia's eyebrows shot up in surprise. "So....I'm hired?" Her voice sounded squeaky to her own ears but she couldn't help it. The idea that anyone would hire her on the spot with no experience or references, well...it seemed like a miracle. Especially when she'd been moments away from calling it quits.

The universe works in mysterious ways, her grandfather would say.

The hot bartender leaned over the bar and clasped his hands. "Let's not get carried away," he said with a laugh. "You're hired on a probationary basis. We're understaffed so I'm allowed to hire a few new people. I'll start you out with some slow shifts and if it works out, you can pick up a normal workload. Deal?"

Lucia nodded. "Deal."

He went to take her application from her but paused when he saw all the blank spaces. "You're going to have to fill in the bare minimum here so we can put you on the payroll."

He pushed the paper back toward her along with the pen but Lucia paused before picking them up. The bartender seemed to notice because he leaned over further and spoke quietly. "Don't worry, the managers here don't dig too deep."

Her head shot up in surprise. Did he know who she was? Her grandfather had always shielded his children and grandchildren from the press but maybe he recognized her from the crazy publicity that surrounded Daniel and Ivy's wedding at the Brunelli estate. It had been impossible to avoid the media frenzy that had descended upon their little town in Tuscany and the Brunelli clan had found itself under a magnifying glass.

"I, uh, I can explain," she started.

The bartender shook his head. "No need. Believe me, you aren't the first person to come in here without working papers and you won't be the last."

Lucia blinked up at him. Working papers? And then it clicked into place. He thought she was worried about filling in her last name because she was in the country illegally. She almost laughed out loud in relief. While she had been raised in Italy, her mother had actually given birth to her in New York at a hospital in the Bronx so Lucia was fortunate enough to have dual citizenship. But there was no need to tell this kind stranger that. So instead she let him see her smile of genuine relief.

"Thank you."

For one brief moment their eyes met and she was sure he knew that she was keeping a secret. And in that split second, she had the overwhelming compulsion to tell this man everything. But then he smiled and the moment was over as he slid the paper out in his direction and snatched the pen out of her hands. "So, let's see here…" he drawled as he perused the blanks spaces.

Lucia let out a little laugh when he bent over the paper and started filling in the top section. "What are you doing?"

He ignored her as he scribbled something on another line.

"There," he said with finality as he slid it back toward her. "You're all set, Lucia."

A laugh bubbled up in her throat as she read his answers. "Lucia… Jones?" She arched a brow in disbelief. "Is that the best you could come up with?"

He shrugged. "What can I say, I'm not terribly creative with my lies. I've always heard that when it comes to lying, the simpler the better."

Lucia's eyes narrowed with mock suspicion. "And do you lie often?"

He plucked a straw from its holder and tossed it at her. "Only for damsels in distress."

That had her outright laughing. "Is that what I am? Here I thought I was the answer to your prayers." As soon as the words were out of her mouth she realized how flirtatious they sounded. Heat crept into her cheeks. "Because you're looking for a waitress, I mean."

His eyes were filled with teasing laughter and she waited for a mocking retort. But instead he let her off easy. "Of course."

Lucia shifted in her seat. She shouldn't be flirting with her new boss. But he was so close and his eyes seemed so kind. It had been a while since anyone had flirted with her. She had been surrounded by women and gay men at the internship, with no time to meet people during her precious off hours. And here was this man, this kind, sexy, gorgeous…nameless man.

Lucia stuck out her hand. "Let's try this again. Hi, I'm Lucia Jones."

He laughed but took her hand in his. "Nice to meet you, Lucia Jones. I'm Ryan Smith."

Chapter 2

The jolt of electricity that shot through Ryan at the touch of her hand made it clear—he was in trouble. Serious trouble.

Lucia's head tilted to the side as she laughed up at him, her long black curls falling over one shoulder. "Seriously?" she said in that adorable Italian accent of hers. "You're going with Smith?"

Ryan shrugged and told another lie. "It's the truth."

Her soft hand was still tucked in his, like it belonged there. He'd been drawn to this sexy siren from the moment she'd stepped foot in his bar— what red-blooded male wouldn't be? And now that he was touching her, he didn't want to let go.

Oh yeah, this was trouble. He forced himself to release her hand and busied himself with wiping down the already clean bar.

What had he been thinking? As if he wasn't in enough danger working for the enemy under a false name, now he went and hired a girl who clearly had baggage of her own. And worse, she was hot. All of the women who worked at the hotel bar tended to be attractive, but this woman was smoldering—a sexy combination of curvaceous sex bomb and innocent girl next door. And she was looking at him now with those big brown eyes filled with gratitude.

But really, what was he supposed to do? The girl had clearly been desperate. She looked about ready to faint from hunger or burst into tears. Ryan wasn't exactly a saint but he couldn't turn her out on the streets... besides, he really *was* desperate to fill a waitressing role.

He needed a waitress and this woman clearly needed a job. It was that simple. He would make sure it stayed that simple. "So when can you start?"

He glanced over in time to see her face light up, her wide eyes bright with excitement. Somehow her reaction seemed to have a direct correlation to his own level of happiness. Pride swept through him at being the one to make her excited. "I can start right away," she said, jumping up out of her chair.

"Whoa, tiger, I've got some paperwork to file and I have to get the okay from my boss—"

Her expectant smile dropped instantly. "I thought I was hired."

"You are. But I have to run it by my bosses. They'll have to meet you." He watched the woman before him transform from an enthusiastic, upbeat new employee to a nervous, self-conscious runaway. If he didn't know better he'd think that she was running away from something...or someone. She couldn't really be a runaway....could she?

He studied her now with the eye of a bartender and not just a man with blood in his veins. He would swear she was over eighteen but better safe than sorry. "How old are you?"

Lucia's nose scrunched up in confusion, which was answer enough. "Twenty-four. I told you that already."

Ryan moved from behind the bar and stood directly in front of her. She was telling the truth about her age, he didn't doubt that, but he hadn't imagined the change in her demeanor either. There was a wariness about her. That, along with the fact that she was lying about her identity could only mean she was on the run. But from what? Or who? He leaned against the bar so his eyes were level with his. "What are you so scared of?"

Her lips curled up in a smile but it didn't extend to her eyes. It was brilliant and dazzling and almost enough to throw him off track—but it was definitely forced.

He watched as she thrust her shoulders back, her chin tilted up in stubborn defiance. "I'm not afraid of anything." Her words were contradicted by the fear he saw in her eyes.

He almost believed her. Almost. Most men would take one look at that dazzling smile and confident posture and take her word for it. But then most men weren't living a lie. It took a liar to know liar, and this woman was hiding something, he would bet his life on it. The thought nagged at him and filled him with a frustrating unease. He wanted to help her but he couldn't save a damsel in distress if she didn't tell him the truth. Letting out a heavy sigh, he had to laugh at his own hypocrisy. Who was he to demand honesty from some woman he'd just met when his life was one giant lie?

Letting her off the hook, he turned back to move behind the bar but a figure lurking near the host stand caught his eye. Despite his desire to shout at the man to get out of his bar, Ryan motioned to the man to stay where he was. Ryan stopped himself from cursing out loud. No need to drag this nice new waitress into his mess.

One of the barbacks came out with a large platter of appetizers and Ryan took it from him, setting it in front of Lucia with a flourish. "Your lunch, madam."

Her laugh was light and sweet as she reached for a chicken finger and then a mozzarella stick, shoving them into her mouth so quickly he had to wonder how long it had been since she last ate. He muttered something about leaving her to eat in peace but he needn't have bothered, she was too engrossed in her meal to even look up.

Keeping a neutral expression on his face for the sake of the busboys and waitstaff who were setting up the tables for dinner, he walked over to the host stand where his older brother was leaning against the wall, texting someone on his phone.

He cleared his throat to get his brother's attention, swallowing down his resentment that his brother was checking up on him. Again. "What are you doing here, Billy?"

Billy took his time finishing his text before looking up at him from below lowered eyebrows, fixing him with a familiar scowl of disapproval that he had come to hate. "The question is, what are *you* doing here?"

Ryan let out the exasperated sigh he'd been holding in since he spotted his brother. They'd been over this countless times. It had been the same story from the moment he'd landed the job at Daniel Gladwell's hotel. Yes, he was here to get vengeance for his family but his brother couldn't seem to comprehend that getting close to the boss took time. It wasn't like he could storm in Daniel's office and demand payback. That was the route Billy and their mother had taken and it had gotten them nothing—well, nothing but restraining orders. This time they'd agreed to try it his way but Billy was too impatient and had never heard the word "subtle" so he supposed he shouldn't be surprised the Billy couldn't understand that getting close to the enemy and finding his weakness was a long game.

Ryan glanced around to make sure no one was paying attention to them and lowered his voice. "You've gotta get out of here. Someone might recognize you."

Billy shook his head. "The only person who could recognize me is Daniel and he's not returning from Chicago until tomorrow."

Of course Billy knew that, he'd been the one to fill Ryan in on his latest trip. According to Billy's source, who his brother refused to name, the ruthless businessman was in Chicago to buy a company out from underneath another sucker, just like he'd done to their father. Billy found the info and he made sure Ryan knew every move Daniel made. He had to if he was going to infiltrate the tycoon's inner circle.

"Still," Ryan said. "You can't be seen lurking around here and talking to me. You look like a goddamn stalker."

Billy's bloated face broke into a mocking smile and stood up straight so he was taller than Ryan. He was six years older than Ryan and even though they were both adults now, Billy still treated him like a little kid.

"I don't need a babysitter," he added.

Billy kept his voice low but his tone was hard. "I think you do. And so does Mom. We give you one little job and poor little Ryan can't hack it."

Billy's taunting tone had Ryan clenching his teeth to keep from losing his cool. "I told you, I just need time."

But Billy wasn't listening, he was looking over Ryan's shoulder to the bar. No, he was leering, and he didn't have to look back to see that his brother was ogling Lucia. "You say you're working on it but so far you've gotten nothing. And then I show up to see what kind of progress you made and find you flirting with some hot guest—"

"She's not a guest," Ryan cut in, although that wasn't the point and he knew it. "She works here."

Billy rolled his eyes. "Please. I can spot a rich chick a mile away. That girl screams entitled brat."

Ryan glanced back at the new waitress who was still devouring her plate of food. An ache slashed through his chest. His brother couldn't drag her into this. She was innocent, defenseless. She had nothing to do with the bitter anger that fueled his family. Before he could come to her defense, his brother continued. "The point is, you're slacking off."

Taking a deep breath, Ryan ordered himself to keep his cool. Losing his temper in front of the staff was a surefire way to gain unwanted attention. "I'm not slacking off," he said through tight lips, "I'm playing the part. Do you really think anyone will buy my 'Ryan Smith' routine if all I do is ask questions and poke around in the offices?"

Billy opened his mouth to protest but Ryan held up a hand to cut him off. "We agreed that I'm the one taking the risk here—I'm the one putting myself in the line of fire—so we do this my way."

Billy glared at Ryan's hand until he let it drop. "Your way is taking too long. It's time we move on to Plan B."

No. Hell no. The only reason he'd agreed to get involved with their revenge plans was to keep Billy and their mother from going too far. As their bitterness grew, their schemes grew more vindictive, more personal. If they did it Ryan's way, Daniel would be the only one to pay. Not his family or his employees…just Daniel. The man who'd ruined their lives. "We agreed we'd try it my way first." Ryan struggled to keep his voice neutral. "Daniel's family shouldn't have to pay for his crimes—not if there's another way. I'll find a way in and I'll do whatever it takes to take him down. You have my word."

Billy studied him with beady eyes – their father's eyes. The older Billy got, the more he resembled their dad. He'd inherited their father's thinning hair, along with a body that was bloated from drinking. "Fine, but stop fawning over the chicks at your bar and keep your head in the game."

Ryan resisted the urge to defend himself once again. He wasn't interested in "the chicks at his bar," as Billy put it. He glanced over at Lucia. Seeing his brother was the perfect reminder of why he didn't date—why he couldn't date. He couldn't drag anyone else into his family's mess.

He watched his brother walk away with relief. Whether he liked it or not, they were in this together. They had both suffered when Daniel bought out their father's business, the business that was supposed to be their birthright. But brothers or not, they had little in common and having a shared goal did nothing to change that.

He let all thoughts of Billy and Daniel and their longstanding feud fade away as he headed back to the bar where his new waitress had already scarfed down most of the contents of the sampler platter. It was hard to resist laughing out loud at her look of shame as she pushed the plate toward him when he returned. "Sorry," she mumbled. "I was really hungry."

He took stock of the two pieces of celery that were left on the ravaged plate. "I wasn't that hungry anyways." His stomach gave a low growl of protest. He was starving, actually, but he didn't want to make her feel worse.

Lucia toyed with her napkin. "So, when should I show up for my first day?"

Ryan pretended to mull it over. He couldn't have her starting tonight, not without getting the okay from his manager, but he hated to see her go. He watched her nibble on her lower lip, waiting for his answer when it dawned on him. He had a crush.

Bloody hell. Just what he needed in his life. As if going undercover as a bartender at Daniel's hotel wasn't enough of a headache, he now had a crush on his new employee. A girl who had secrets of her own and no clue who he really was. Life had been complicated before but now, thanks to this hottie at his bar, he was playing with fire.

To Lucia, he said, "Come back tomorrow, we'll start your training at five."

* * * *

Lucia was hit with a wave of jealousy when she returned to her temporary studio apartment in Brooklyn to find her roommate knee-deep in clothes as she attempted to shove the contents of her life into an oversized duffel bag.

Gretchen glanced up when she walked in. "How'd it go? Did he give you the money?"

Lucia pushed away the envy that threatened to drown her as she dropped onto the futon that doubled as the girls' shared bed. She should be happy. Compared to this morning, things were looking up. She was staying in New York and that was something to celebrate. With that in mind, she forced a cheerful tone. "Better. I got a job!"

Gretchen dropped down into a cross-legged sitting position facing Lucia. The two girls had met when Lucia joined Eleanor's entourage for Fashion Week. Gretchen was trying to make a name for herself in the hair and makeup world just like she was attempting to establish herself as an up-and-coming designer. The two had formed an alliance when it became clear that they were both newbies with no money.

Gretchen stared at her with wide eyes. "You got signed on with another designer? That's amazing! Does that mean you're coming to London with us?"

Lucia's smile faltered but she reminded herself once again that this was a good thing….maybe not the best possible scenario but it beat going home to her grandfather and worse, her ex-fiancé, admitting defeat.

"No," she said slowly. "Actually, I'll be waitressing. At a hotel bar."

Gretchen seemed to deflate a bit but she did a decent job of hiding her disappointment. "Oh. Well, that's….good. Right?"

"Yes," Lucia said a little too quickly. "It's great. It means I can stay in New York."

Gretchen perked up. "You could take classes at FIT."

"Exactly." Lucia could only imagine how expensive those classes were and after the end of this month, she would be paying full rent for the tiny studio. The classes would have to wait. But she could work on her own designs in her free time and maybe eventually she could save up for a class or two. Or maybe find an internship. Gretchen started folding a pile of clothes beside her while casting quick glances in Lucia's direction.

"Are you sure you know what you're doing?"

No. But she would figure it out, she promised herself. She'd come this far, she wouldn't turn back now. Not when a hot bartender came to her rescue and gave her a chance to stay in NYC and pursue her dreams. She just needed time. Her grandfather hadn't raised a quitter.

Besides, Gretchen worrying about her from London wouldn't help anything. So Lucia gave a decisive nod. "Positive."

Gretchen leaned back against the side of the bed with a sigh. "Why can't we all just be filthy rich? Then you could not only come with us to London, but you could have a show of your own."

Lucia's stomach sank. She hated that she'd been lying to her new friend since the moment they'd met. But then, how could she explain to Gretchen that she came from wealth...but walked away from it?

Besides, what difference did it make? It wasn't like she had the money *now*.

"It takes more than just money to become a world-class designer," Lucia said.

Gretchen rolled her eyes. "Duh. It takes talent. Which you have. Even Eleanor said she thought you had what it takes to make it. And she never gives compliments."

Lucia grinned at her friend. Eleanor *had* said that and she'd replayed the famous designer's words over and over in her mind. It had been exactly the boost of confidence she'd needed. Eleanor's confidence had been a balm to her wounded pride after spending so many years defending her desire to go into the fashion industry, a profession her ex-fiancé had deemed superficial and her grandfather had relegated to a hobby.

Gretchen dove back into her pile of clothes with a theatrical sigh. "Now if only you could get your hands on a couple hundred grand— you'd have it made."

Lucia laughed at her friend's teasing but she couldn't bring herself to look her in the eyes. She had that much money—actually she had far more than that—she just didn't have access to it. If any of her new friends knew how much she was worth, would they still welcome her into their fold?

She brushed the thought away. *No use dwelling in what-ifs*, that's what Grandpa always said. The same Grandpa who was probably worried sick about her. Jack and Holly had given him an update and she'd sent the occasional email to let him know she was alive and well—but still, she knew him. He was probably taking out his worry on her little cousins, not letting them out of his sight for fear they might follow in her footsteps.

"Hey, what came over you?" Gretchen asked. "I thought we were celebrating. You look like someone killed your cat."

Lucia frowned. "I don't have a cat."

Gretchen ignored that. Instead, she leaned toward Lucia, her eyes narrowed with suspicion. "Does this have anything to do with that guy who was asking about you at the after party last night?"

Lucia froze. But she was overreacting, surely. No one was looking for her. No one even knew who she was. But still…. "What guy?"

Gretchen shrugged. "He showed up after you left—why did you leave so early anyways?"

Lucia resisted the urge to groan at her friend's tendency to get sidetracked. "Gretchen," she said. "Describe this guy."

Over the next few moments, one thing became clear. Gretchen was not terribly observant.

"Tall with dark hair?" Lucia repeated after what felt like an eternity. "That's all you remember?"

Gretchen tucked a stray lock of blond hair behind her ear. "Sorry, I'd had a couple cocktails."

Which, Lucia knew from firsthand experience, was Gretchen's code for quite a lot of cocktails. She should consider herself lucky her roommate remembered him at all. Lucia went through all of the possibilities. Who would be asking about her?

"What did he say? Did he ask for me by name?" Her fingers tightened around the pillow she was holding. What if this stranger knew her secret? What if he knew who she was?

Gretchen nodded. "He definitely asked if I knew where Lucia had gone."

Lucia's breath caught in her throat. "Did he use a last name?"

Gretchen's face scrunched up in confusion, probably in response to Lucia's admittedly intense tone more than anything. But she had gone to quite a bit of trouble to ensure that no one knew her last name. If she was going to avoid her mother's mistakes, it was critical that no one knew who she really was. Or, rather, who her family was. After all, she couldn't fall victim to a gold digger if no one knew she had gold, right? Gretchen was still looking at her as though she'd lost her mind because of course she had no idea that her new friend was a runaway heiress. Lucia did her best to relax and feign nonchalance. "I mean, do you happen to remember how he referred to me? I'm wondering how well he knows me…."

Her roommate turned back to her task at hand, clearly losing interest in this game of twenty questions. "I don't know, I think he said 'Lucia'…or maybe 'Lucy'? I don't know, I can't remember."

Lucy? Could it be Marco? He was the only one who ever called her Lucy. The thought of her ex-fiancé being nearby...of being on the same *continent*, was enough to send her into an emotional tailspin.

They had been together so long—forever, it seemed. He was the boy next door, her partner for every dance, her first kiss, her first everything. He'd always been there. As much a part of her life as her grandfather and her cousins. Leaving him behind had been painful.

But she didn't regret her decision. She knew in her gut that she'd done what was best for both of them. They didn't want the same things. He wanted a wife who would devote herself to him and their future family. Someone who would be content to stay in their little village in Tuscany and follow in their parents' footsteps. Well, *his* parents' footsteps. Certainly no one wanted her to follow her mother's path, least of all her. In her defense, she'd tried to want all of that. She spent her entire life trying to want the future that Marco and her grandfather wanted for her. Lucia followed the rules, she played the part of the dutiful girlfriend and granddaughter...until she just couldn't pretend any longer.

Maybe she really was her mother's daughter.

Lucia shook that thought off with a flip of her hair. She was nothing like her mother. True, they'd both run away to America but she would never be so foolish as to fall for a loser playboy and get knocked up. She was here for one thing and one thing only – the one thing Marco could never support – the career of her dreams.

Marco had made his objections to her dreams clear. The more he brushed off her dreams like they were nonsensical fluff that could be dismissed with a pat on the head, the more she pushed back, unable to let the topic drop. It had taken time before she realized that Marco – her Marco, who had been her constant companion – truly didn't believe that she had what it took to make a career a reality. He couldn't even understand why she would want to.

She leaned back with a sigh. No, there was no doubt in her mind that she had made the right decision in calling off their wedding. Yet there was still a part of her that felt like a limb was missing. And if he was here in New York City? What would she say? What would she do? But how would he know how to find her? Holly and Jack had sworn that they wouldn't tell anyone she was here—except her grandfather.

Her heart rate started to return to a normal rate as she reasoned and rationalized her way to sanity. It was probably just some guy who she'd met through work. Maybe she did have a secret admirer after all.

Gretchen had moved on from the mystery man conversation and was instead giving Lucia a play by play of all of the designers and stylists she'd be working alongside at the London show.

Lucia smiled and laughed along with her friend and tried to ignore the jealousy that left a bitter taste in her mouth. She should be happy for her new friend—and she was. She just wished that she could go too.

"Maybe you'll save up enough to come join us," Gretchen said. Her friend's eyes were filled with sympathy.

Maybe Lucia hadn't done such a stellar job of disguising her jealousy after all.

"Maybe," Lucia said with what she hoped was an optimistic smile. *Probably not.* She'd never waited tables before but something told her whatever money she made would barely cover the full rent for the studio she was subletting, let alone add up to enough for airfare to England.

"We could share a flat again if you can get enough money to come over," Gretchen insisted.

Lucia nodded. She wanted to speak but she was afraid if she tried, she would start to cry. It was so unfair. She'd given up everything to go chasing after her dreams. And six weeks later she had to call it quits... because she'd failed.

Or maybe her grandfather and Marco had been right all along and she was just too naïve. Maybe believing that hard work and passion were enough to bring about success was childish. *It's time to grow up, Lucy.* Marco's parting words played in a loop in her head. Being an adult, for Marco, meant following the well-laid plans ahead of them. It meant following the color-by-number pattern formed by his parents and her grandparents' expectations. She would get a cushy, well-paid job at her grandfather's company, at least until she got pregnant, and Marco would pursue his dreams of being a doctor. Done and done.

Except that Lucia had no say in any of it. All those years she'd blindly followed the rules and did as she was expected. She didn't want to rock the boat, like her mother had done.

But then she had. Calling off the engagement and running away to New York City was more than rocking the boat. She had shipwrecked the damn thing.

Gretchen stood up from her mountain of clothes and shifted to sit beside Lucia on the bed. Throwing an arm around her shoulder, she gave Lucia a little side hug. "Cheer up, *chica.* You've got the talent and the drive....you just need a little money and you'll blow them all away with your very own collection."

Lucia gave a little snort of disbelief at that understatement. "A *little* money?"

Gretchen laughed. "Okay, maybe a big boatload of money. But it'll happen. You're the one who's always saying, we just need to pay our dues and all of our dreams will come true."

Lucia tried not to wince at having her own words tossed back in her face. She was the first to admit sometimes her optimism walked the line between sweet and annoying.

"It may take a while, but we're both going to get there eventually."

Eventually. Five years and nine months, to be exact. Lucia summoned a smile for her friend. Gretchen, apparently heartened by the effect her little pep talk was having, continued on with vigor. "And just think, in ten years from now maybe you and I will have enough money saved up to put on a show of our own. We'll start small, obviously…"

As her roommate continued to plan out their budget-friendly first show a decade in the future, Lucia struggled to avoid a tidal wave of guilt.

Marco had been right. During that awful last fight, he'd told her she was a spoiled, entitled princess. That was exactly what she was. Here she was crying to her friend about not having money to make her dreams come true—but at least she had the promise of a trust fund. Granted, she couldn't touch it for years but at least she knew it was coming, along with all of the freedom and opportunities money provided. Gretchen, meanwhile, had no such fallback—no promise of a windfall coming down the road.

Humbled by this realization, Lucia wrapped her arms around Gretchen and squeezed tight. "I really am happy for you, you know. You deserve this break. And you're going to be a world-class, in-demand stylist in no time."

Gretchen laughed as Lucia pulled back and jumped up, pulling Gretchen to her feet alongside her. "Come on, let's finish packing you up so we can send you off in style."

One hour and three suitcases later, Gretchen's life was packed and sitting in wait by the front door. Their little farewell party consisted of a pan of brownies and the cheapest bottle of wine they could find at the liquor store, which thoroughly depleted the rest of Lucia's life savings.

Thank goodness she was starting a new job the next day.

She lay in bed that night, too full of sugar and nerves over her first day of work to actually sleep. If her grandfather could see her now, he would be laughing his head off. The fact that she was grateful and excited about starting a waitressing job would have been inconceivable a mere month before.

She grinned up at the ceiling as an image of bright blue eyes and unbelievably sexy dimples flashed before her. But then again…she hadn't met the outrageously hot bartender back then either.

Chapter 3

Ryan's barback tossed a twenty-dollar bill onto the bar. "Twenty bucks says the new waitress doesn't show."

Ryan pushed the money back. "She'll be here," he said with more confidence than he felt. She was only ten minutes late.

"Are we talking about the same girl?" Javier asked. He wiped down the ice bin and glanced back at Ryan over his shoulder. "That chick who showed up early yesterday was a hottie, and I'd swear on my life she comes from money."

Ryan stopped counting the money in the till and turned to his friend. Javier's words were almost the exact repeat of his brother's. "The girl didn't have enough money to buy herself some lunch, Jav. Besides, how many people do you know apply for waiting gigs for the fun of it?"

Javier shook his head, "She was wearing clothes my sister would drool over and had that look...." Javier stuck his nose up in the air and cocked his head to the side so he was looking down at Ryan. "You know the look."

Ryan had to laugh at Javier's impersonation. "Trust me, she may hold herself like royalty but if you could have heard her talk or seen the look in her eyes...." Ryan shook his head. "The girl looked scared."

Javier straightened at that. "Scared? Of what?"

Ryan shrugged. He hadn't been able to stop thinking about Lucia from the moment she'd walked out of his bar. He couldn't put his finger on it, but something about her and her situation made him uneasy. She'd been nervous and shady—two things that should have set off alarms. The last thing he needed was to get involved with a girl who had secrets of her own. But instead of alarms, he'd heard a goddamn siren song.

The girl had gotten into his head and he had no idea how...or why. All he knew was, he wanted to help her. He wanted to swoop in and save the day. Ryan laughed at his own delusional thoughts. He was nothing more than a liar and a con man, not exactly the white knight to her damsel in distress.

"What's so funny, man?" Javier asked.

Ryan shook his head. "Nothing. Just do me a favor, and be nice to Lucia when she shows up."

"*If* she shows up," Javier added.

Ryan rolled his eyes but let it slide. "I'm serious."

Javier leaned against the ice bin and started the slow and tedious process of wiping down the glassware. "Why? Do you like this girl or something? Does someone have a crush on the *principessa*?"

Ryan ignored the teasing and made a show of counting the ones, even though he'd long since lost track of what number he was on. "I'm just saying, she's in this country illegally and she needs a job." He glanced up to see his friend studying the glass he was holding. "I think she's afraid of getting deported, she was really skittish when it came to giving her personal info."

Ryan saw that his comment had struck a chord by his friend's sudden silence. Only six months before, Javier had been in a similar position. Now he had his green card, but he'd been flying below the radar for years before he eventually got it. Javier cursed beneath his breath. "Yeah, all right, I'll play nice."

They both turned as Lucia flew into the bar area, her long black waves pulled into a loose ponytail and wearing a simple, black T-shirt and pants. "I'm so sorry," she said. "I couldn't find my Metrocard and I didn't have enough for a new one and—"

Ryan held up a hand to stop the rush of words. "It's fine. You're only ten minutes late."

Lucia set her bag down with a loud exhale and flashed Ryan and Javier a brilliant smile. "So...where should I get started?"

Ryan swiped the twenty from the bar while giving Javier a not-so-subtle "I told you so" look.

Javier gave him the finger behind the bar, out of sight from Lucia, but then he turned to her with a warm smile and motioned for her to follow him into the kitchen. "Come with me, I'll give you a tour of the back of house and then Ryan here can show you the ropes."

Showing Lucia the ropes was, in a word, painful. The girl was eager to learn but quite possibly the most inexperienced worker he'd ever met. He had his doubts about whether she'd ever stepped foot in an actual kitchen when he had to explain how a dishwasher worked but when he watched her cleaning the tables, it was obvious that she was not familiar with manual labor.

"Have you even seen a dish rag before?"

He was watching her wipe down a table by pushing the rag around with the tips of her fingers like she was afraid the dirty cloth would bite her. She looked over with a mock scowl before setting her jaw and attacking the table with vigor. Ryan resisted the urge to laugh.

He shouldn't tease her, not when she was so clearly making an effort to learn. At least she was trying, although he was fairly certain he was going to have to re-roll the silverware before the rest of the waitstaff arrived for their shift.

When she finished scrubbing down the last table, she came back to the bar to find him looking more than a little pleased with herself. "What's next, boss?"

She cocked one hip against the bar and rested her fist against her hip, letting the dirty rag dangle from her belt loop like the barbacks who were already prepping the bar. Ryan didn't know if he was going to laugh at her enthusiasm or excuse himself to go take a cold shower.

The girl was hot. There was no denying it. She'd been sexy in a sweet, girl-next-door kind of way when she'd sat at his bar the day before with her prim and proper sundress and cardigan. But here, now, with her long, black wavy hair slipping out of the ponytail to frame her heart-shaped face and those almond-brown eyes blinking up with him with unbelievably long lashes....this was no girl next door. The black clothes clung to her curves in all the right places and the V-neck top revealed just enough cleavage to make breathing difficult.

But it was those lips that nearly caused him to lose his mind. Luscious and pink and perfectly pouting, even now, when a small smile tilted up the corners. He couldn't seem to tear his eyes away, even when she nudged him. "So, am I done with my training? Am I that good?"

Her teasing tone brought Ryan back to his sense and his gaze managed to tear itself away from temptation as he focused on the lime he was cutting. "Oh yeah, you're a natural."

His sarcasm was not lost on Lucia. The pouting lips actually did pout then.

He should never have glanced back at temptation. The moment he did, the knife in his hand slipped off the surface of the lime and nicked his thumb.

"Dammit." Grabbing a clean towel, he wrapped the minor lust-wound while he searched for the first-aid kit with its endless supply of Band-Aids.

"Here, let me help you." Lucia was on her hands and knees beside him, trying to find it in the cluttered shelves behind the bar.

Ryan stopped breathing and instead of saying "I got it," all he managed was a small choking sound.

Her T-shirt was gaping open as she leaned over, giving him a glimpse of her cleavage and the top of her lacy bra. Her breasts were perfection. And he was instantly hard.

"Are you all right?" Lucia was eyeing him with concern.

Fixing his gaze on her forehead—her beautiful, but safe forehead—he decided then and there that hiring Lucia had been a mistake. He couldn't concentrate on a piece of fruit when she was around, how the hell was he going to plot a revenge scheme?

Lucia rose when he did and Ryan put a few feet of sanity-saving distance between them. Focusing on the act of finding the right bandage and fumbling with the wrapping, he studiously avoided eye contact with any part of Lucia. "Look, Lucia, you seem like a really nice girl but I'm not sure this waitressing position is going to work out."

He looked up at the sound of her gasp and immediately wished he'd stuck with his plan to avoid eye contact. Her eyes were wide and sad and, oh God, were those tears?

"I'll help you find another position in the hotel," he quickly added. "I'm sure we can find you something that will be a better fit—maybe at the front desk or at the reservations line."

Lucia's perfect lips twisted to the side a bit as she turned her attention to the bandage in his hand. Effortlessly peeling off the wrapping, she took his hand in hers and leaned in close. He caught one whiff of her citrus-flavored shampoo and the warm, sunny scent that seemed to radiate from her and promptly held his breath.

He was dangerously close to losing control after a few hours of being in close proximity with this woman. His patience was at an all-time low.

Her voice was soft and sad as she wrapped his finger with gentle, delicate movements. "Was I really that bad?"

And with that, all thoughts of his own desire or discomfort were washed away as he hurried to make things right. To make her feel better. "No," he said. He reached out a hand to touch her shoulder but pulled back at the last minute.

She glanced up then with one brow raised in disbelief. "Really?"

Having finished with the bandage, she went to pull her hands from his but his fingers closed around hers, holding them tight. Her eyes widened and she glanced up at him.

Was it his imagination or had she stopped breathing too? For a moment, everything stopped. Time stood still. And then Javier called out a crude joke to one of the busboys who'd shown up late and the moment was over.

Letting out his breath on a long exhale, Ryan turned her hands over so they were both looking at her palms. "You're not bad, you're just inexperienced. I mean, look at these hands." He held them up to the light and he and Lucia both stared at her perfectly manicured hands as though they could read her future. "These are not the hands of a woman who slings drinks or waits on drunk businessmen."

Lucia pulled back her hands. "I know I don't have experience, but I promise I'll learn."

Her pleading tone was heartbreaking. Before he could argue, she continued, her eyes wide and filled with unshed tears. "Please, Ryan. I need this job. I promise I'll work hard and I'll be here on time and I will get callouses and not complain and I'll wait on drunk businessmen and—"

"Look, I get it, you're willing to work hard. But there are a lot of girls who need this job and—"

"I need this job. Please don't make me go home." The words came out abruptly and Ryan got the feeling she didn't intend to say it by the look of surprise on her face. But she recovered quickly and hurried on, "I'm not supposed to be here but I can't go home."

"Is this because you're here illegally?"

Lucia froze for a moment with her mouth partially open and he watched her struggle for words, until she finally said, "Yes. I'm not supposed to be here and there are people who want to send me back. But I can't. Not yet. Okay?"

Ryan watched fear and desperation flicker in her warm, brown eyes and knew that he would say and do just about anything to make them disappear. He exhaled on a sigh. He'd never stood a chance. "Okay, fine. We'll give it a week. If you don't catch on by then…." He let the words trail off, partly because the threat was unnecessary but mainly because her radiant smile had completely wiped away every word in his vocabulary.

"Thank you, thank you, thank you." He watched her whirl away, the dishrag twirling like a tutu as she headed toward the serving station to learn the computer system from Javier.

* * * *

Unfortunately for Ryan, Lucia's second shift was also….not good. His manager had agreed to let him to hire whomever he chose on a probationary basis but also made clear that if his new hires failed, it would be on him to fire them. His job was on the line as much as his new hire's and he couldn't afford to lose this job, not if he wanted to see through his plan. He was here for one reason and one reason only—to get revenge. Having Lucia here was not only a distraction for him but could cost him everything. So why couldn't he bring himself to fire her? If he was smart, he would let her go.

Javier came up to him at one point in the evening and they both watched as she fumbled and then smashed a wine glass. The third one of the night.

"Seriously, man, is this some sort of prank?" Javier asked, his face screwed up in honest confusion. "Are we on camera?"

Ryan shook his head with a sigh. "I don't think so, Jav. This is all her."

"Too bad, I hate to see a hottie go." With those wise and tactful words, Javier walked away leaving Ryan to cringe at the scene.

Javier's words hit home. It wasn't just his job that was at stake by keeping Lucia on—her ineptitude was affecting the rest of the staff as well. It wasn't fair to them to keep on someone who couldn't pull her weight.

He would do it. He'd fire her. But as quickly the thought formed, he dismissed it. He couldn't stop thinking about how excited she'd been to get this job, how happy to have a second chance, and most of all, how scared she'd looked at the thought of having to leave. He couldn't do that to her. She clearly needed this job, even if she couldn't or wouldn't share her reasons.

There had to be another way—a way to keep her on board without risking his job or alienating the rest of the staff. Holding his breath, he watched her juggle a tray before finally steadying it before it tipped into a patron's lap. She needed help, clearly. The girl was a novice in a restaurant but that didn't mean she couldn't be trained. She needed a little extra time and attention, that was all.

He called one of the barbacks over and told him to pass along a message to Lucia that she should stick around after her shift so he could talk to her. The barback nodded with a sympathetic pat on the back and Ryan saw exactly what was going through the younger man's head. He thought Lucia was about to get fired.

Because really, if he was a better manager—and a better brother and son, for that matter—that was exactly what he would do. But not today. Not if there was some other way. And hopefully with a little one-on-one training, she'd get the hang of it. The mere thought of being alone with her that night had his pants tightening against his crotch.

But no, that's not what this was about. This had nothing to do with attraction. And he certainly wasn't looking for an excuse to be alone with her.

He clung to that thought until the last staff member left and he was alone with Lucia. At that precise moment, when she turned to him with those wide brown eyes in the empty bar, he realized he'd been lying to himself. Of course he'd wanted to get her alone. Yes, he wanted to help her, and yes, this could quite possibly be the best way to save her job. But he would have been lying to himself if he hadn't been aching for some time alone with her. He would have settled for a few seconds without the prying eyes of their fellow staff or the nosy bar patrons.

And now here they were. Alone. At last.

Get a grip, Ryan.

"You wanted to see me?" she asked, settling in on a stool at the end of the bar.

He handed her a tray and some glasses. "Show me how you're loading your tray."

She looked from the glasses and back up at him with a questioning look. "Is this a test?"

"Not a test." He laughed. "A lesson. We need to improve some basic waiting skills if you're going to last past the probation period."

At that her eyes widened and she licked her lips nervously.

He resisted the urge to groan out loud. How could he politely tell her not to lick her lips because it drove him crazy....in a good way? Not exactly a work-friendly conversation.

Work. This was about work. Stay focused.

She started loading the tray and he stopped her. "There's the problem. You want to put the heaviest and tallest glasses in the middle to center the weight." She did as she was told and looked up for approval.

"Perfect." He stepped out from behind the bar so he could stand next to her. "Then when you lift the tray you want to put your palm here, in the center and spread your fingers to keep it balanced." He handed it over to her and it immediately started to tip. He helped her steady it and then moved his hand to cover hers so he could nudge it into the correct position.

Bad idea. Very, very bad idea. A sweat broke out on his forehead at the electric awareness that arced between them. He moved away quickly and she flashed him a wide grin as the tray stayed in place on her hand.

"Thanks," she gushed. "That's so much easier to handle." She walked slowly toward the tables and then spun around, keeping the tray perfectly balanced. Her eyes widened with excitement as she made her way back to him without breaking a single glass. "Seriously, thank you."

He shrugged. "No problem. There are lots of little tricks like that that'll make the job easier. You'll pick them up in time."

She sat back down at the bar. "Did you have a lot of experience before you worked here?"

Her arm brushed against his and the jolt of awareness had him moving behind the bar, where he was safe from any unsettling contact. "I waited tables throughout high school and college so, yeah, I guess I've got some experience. I took a break from it when I got my MBA but I guess it's true what they say…it's like riding a bike."

She leaned over the bar and suddenly his plan to keep control by standing back there backfired. Her restaurant-issued crisp white shirt gaped open just enough to give him a tantalizing glimpse of her cleavage. It was enough to make his head spin.

"You got your MBA?" she asked, her voiced filled with eager enthusiasm. "That's impressive. My grandfather is dying for me to go to business school."

Impressive? Hardly. Not when he'd walked away from a promising entry-level position at the insistence of his family. As if reading his mind, Lucia asked, "Why are you still tending bar if you got your business degree?"

Excellent question.

"I, uh…." He'd been lying long enough to know that sticking as close to the truth as possible was the easiest way to lie. "My family fell on some hard times. They lost everything."

Lucia's pouty lips turned into a sympathetic frown.

"They needed me to help."

She made a murmuring sound of understanding. "So you went back to the service industry for the money to save your family?"

More like, for revenge, but who was he to correct her? Besides, his revenge plan was ultimately to get the money that his family deserved— that they *needed*—so it wasn't exactly a lie. "Someone had to."

At her questioning look, he added, "My family used to own a manufacturing company—it was really successful back in the day, but my father lost it shortly before he died." *Lost it.* As if it was a set of keys. More like, had it stolen out from underneath him by a greedy shark named Daniel Gladwell. "My mother, brother, and I were left with nothing."

"That must have been hard, to lose your father and the sense of security all at once."

A familiar resentment made his next words come out gruffer than intended. "It was hard to lose my dad but the money…I don't know, sometimes I think it was for the best." He picked up the rag and rubbed at a sticky spot at the bar with more force than necessary.

His mother and brother didn't see it that way, of course, but growing up the only poor kid on the Upper East Side while his mother tried to cling to their status had left him with a bad taste in him mouth. He'd watched his mother throw herself at their father's wealthy friends, watched his brother try so hard to fit in with the other kids at their school. The ones who weren't there with the help of grants and scholarships. No matter how hard his brother tried—no matter how hard *he'd* tried, they were never accepted by that crowd. When Daniel took the company, he took everything. Their father, their social lives, their place in the world...

Ryan shook his head. His mother and brother were prone to self-pity. He'd opted to make the best of their situation. "Better to grow up learning how to manage in the real world than be a spoiled rich kid with nothing but dreams, right?"

When he looked up her hands were clutched to her chest and her eyes were wide with surprise and something else...hurt, maybe? Oh God, please don't let it be pity. What was he doing spilling his family's dirty laundry? For a moment there he'd nearly forgotten where he was and why he was there. Time to change the topic.

"What about you?" he asked. "What brings you to the wonderful world of waitressing?"

She met his gaze. "You're here to save your family and I'm here to escape mine," she said a little too breezily.

Leaning against the bar, he tried to read her expression but she looked away from him. Alarm bells went off. How much trouble was this girl in? "What are you running from?"

Lucia didn't answer. She turned back in his direction but the only sign that she'd heard him was her lips puckering as if she was struggling with what to say.

"Is there someone looking for you? Someone you need to avoid?"

He shouldn't press her, he knew that, but he couldn't help himself. Every instinct in him wanted to protect her and the longer she remained silent, the more convinced he was that she was in real danger. An abusive boyfriend waiting back in Italy, maybe? A stalker who wouldn't leave her alone? His imagination was doing a hell of a job filling in the blanks, especially when she turned those wide eyes to him and he saw the struggle there. She wanted to talk to him, she wanted to share her secrets. So what was stopping her?

"You can tell me the truth," he said.

That earned him a smile, along with a sad sigh. "Trust me, you don't want to hear it. Besides, I hardly know you."

He covered his heart with his hands as if wounded. "What am I a stranger? And here I thought teaching you how to use the espresso maker was a bonding moment. I'm crushed."

He was relieved to see her eyes sparkling once again. "How well do I really know you, *Mr. Smith*?" Her eyes narrowed teasingly, "If that's really your name."

"It's not." He surprised himself with that one but she laughed out loud.

"So we're both liars then." She raised one brow. "Don't suppose you want to tell me your secrets?"

He couldn't help himself. He gave in to temptation and leaned over the bar so they were nearly touching and adopted the same teasing tone. "I'll tell you mine if you tell me yours."

Her bright, beautiful smile was a sucker punch and he found himself struggling to breathe. "Fair enough. No secrets tonight," she said as she stood and headed toward the exit. "Goodnight, Mr. Smith."

* * * *

So maybe she wasn't the best waitress of all time. Okay, maybe she was a disaster. But at least Ryan had taught her how to properly load up a tray full of drinks so tonight there was no way she would spill another round of beers onto the laps of her customers.

Nope, not tonight

Admittedly, the first two nights had been a bit…disastrous. But tonight, she was pretty sure she was getting the hang of it. She had to be. She only had a few shifts left to show Ryan that she could do this. And she needed this job. She also wanted this job—and not just for the money. Well, the money was a big part of it—who else would hire her, giving her a chance to stay in NYC? But she also hated the idea of saying goodbye to her new bartender friend.

Lucia glanced over to see Ryan eyeing her tray warily. Lucia made a show of rolling her eyes and glided toward the table that was patiently waiting for drinks. Setting each drink down carefully, she couldn't resist turning back to gloat.

But Ryan's back was turned as he poured a draught beer and her attention was caught by a familiar man leaning against the bar, typing on his phone.

Her heart gave a little stutter as recognition set in. She could have sworn she'd seen him before.

Yes, she was positive. That was the guy she'd seen at her last runway show with Eleanor. She remembered because he'd looked as out of place there with his cheap suit as he did at this high-end hotel bar. She was almost certain she'd spotted him outside her apartment building a couple of days ago and again in Prospect Park when she'd gone for a jog.

She'd been starting to think she was paranoid but now here he was... again. At her bar. What were the odds? Her mind was racing to figure out what why this man was following her, but no matter how she looked at it, there was no way she could pretend that this man was interested in Lucia Jones. No—he was looking for Lucia Brunelli.

Heart racing, Lucia dropped her tray at the nearest serving station and slipped into the back hallway leading to the kitchen, where she could stare at the mystery man without being seen.

Javier's voice behind her made her jump. "Your shift only started an hour ago and you're hiding already?"

"I'm not hiding, I'm—" She forgot her excuse when the mystery man looked up from his phone and turned back to the restaurant. He was clearly looking for someone—for *her*.

Javier stood beside her now. "Who are we watching?" He followed her gaze. "Oh, that guy? Looks kinda shady, right? He was in here last night too."

Lucia turned to him, her blood freezing in her veins. "He was?"

"Yeah, he came in late. We told him we were closed." Javier looked from the man and back to her, his brows drawn together in confusion. "What's the deal, do you know this guy or something?"

Lucia shook her head. "No, but...I think he's here for me."

Javier's brows shot up in surprise. "What for?"

Lucia opened her mouth but no words came out. That was what she needed to figure out. Javier was waiting for her to speak but what could she say? He may be a tabloid reporter who's tracked down the missing Italian heiress. Or maybe he'd been sent by her grandfather or by her former fiancé whom she'd practically left at the altar. Any answer she gave would only lead to more questions and she needed to make some phone calls to get to the bottom of this.

"Ummm," she started.

Javier's look of interest was rapidly turning to concern. "Lucia, what is it? Who is this guy?"

Lucia flashed the excuse that Ryan had given her that first day and she couldn't give him her name. "Immigration."

Her mouth clamped shut. Did that even make sense? Javier's eyes narrowed for a moment as he studied her in apparent confusion and she found herself mimicking his look until suddenly—and unexpectedly—his stance loosened and he was nodding in understanding.

"Don't sweat it. Stay out of sight for a while, I'll cover your tables."

Javier walked off when Lucia stared after him with a looming sense of guilt. That had been too easy. And wrong. Oh so wrong. A number of the servers and back of house staff had issues with immigration and to use their real plight for her own selfish reasons....

But now was not the time to worry about moral dilemmas—not when she had a mystery man stalking her. Holly was the first person she dialed. Daniel's sister-in-law and Jack's girlfriend, Holly could always be counted on to spill if she knew anything.

"Lucia!"

Lucia grinned at Holly's high-pitched screech of excitement on the other end of the line. "How are you? Wait, *where* are you? Are you still in New York? Are you coming back to Europe soon because I swear to God, it's not the same without you."

Lucia cut in before her friend could get carried away. "I'm still in New York. And loving it. But, I need to ask you something...."

She heard Jack laughing about something in the background before Holly loudly shushed him. "Shoot."

In a few short sentences, Lucia explained her situation—leaving out the parts about being woefully broke and working at the bar in Daniel's hotel. When she was done, she heard Holly's sigh. "I told your grandfather to stop worrying...."

"You think Grandpa is behind this?"

"It wouldn't surprise me," Holly said. "Jack and I told him you were doing fine on your own in New York, but you know how he worries."

Lucia rolled her eyes at the understatement even though her friend couldn't see her. Her grandfather had raised her after her mother passed away when she was a baby. Her father had never been on the scene and her grandmother passed away when she was little so she was raised almost singlehandedly by her grandfather, along with a slew of housekeepers, nannies, and her aunts and uncles. But despite the army of people who'd surrounded her, it was he who had always worried about her the most.

Probably because he was afraid she would turn out like her mother. Whether it was conscious or not, she'd picked up on that fear at a young age and spent most of her life trying to be everything her mother was not. She'd been the perfect daughter he'd never had. Until she wasn't. She'd destroyed his trust when she'd gone and done *exactly* what her mother had done. She'd run away to America, just like her. She shook off that thought. This was different. She wouldn't make the same mistakes. Her mother had been blinded by love—but luckily for Lucia, she hadn't inherited her mother and grandfather's romantic tendencies. She was practical, like her grandmother. How did her grandfather not see that? His lack of faith in her was more than a little insulting.

"You really think he hired someone to follow me?" Lucia asked. The thought irritated her but at least it was less creepy than having a stalker. Lucia was nothing if not an optimist.

"I don't know, I mean, Jack and I made him swear to leave you alone but…you know your grandfather." Holly didn't have to say anything more. She knew her grandpa better than most. He could swear up and down that he would give her the freedom she so desperately craved, but he didn't get where he was by caving to other people's wishes.

If there was one the he was good at, it was rationalizing. She could just see him now, telling himself that he was respecting her wishes by giving her the *illusion* that she was really free. Meanwhile, he'd hired her a babysitter!

"Lucia? You still there?"

"Yeah." Lucia drew in a deep breath and tried not to let the anger color her voice. It wasn't Holly's fault that her grandfather was up to his usual tricks.

"Do you want me to call him?" Holly asked. "Jack and I can talk some sense into him if he's playing mother hen."

Mother hen. A reluctant smile tugged at her lips at that accurate description. An overbearing, melodramatic, control freak of a mother hen. "No, I've got this."

"You sure?" Jack had apparently snatched the phone from Holly because now his concerned voice could be heard on the other end of the line. "I can give him a call."

"No," Lucia said. "Thanks, but I can handle my grandfather."

She said her goodbyes to Holly and Jack. Anger and adrenaline coursed through her at the thought of her grandfather's manipulative and overbearing ways. How dare he swear to give her space and then have her *followed*?

She was barely aware of the dining patrons or the busy waitstaff that moved around her as she headed toward the mystery man her grandfather had sent. He had turned back to the bar as she was approaching and didn't see her come near.

"Can I help you?" Lucia asked the man's back.

He turned around so quickly he nearly knocked over his drink and Lucia was gratified to see him at a temporary loss for words. Had an actual interaction with her not been part of her grandfather's plan? Good. Nothing annoyed him more than having his plans thwarted.

She crossed her arms and stared up at the tall, shabby patron with brows raised in expectation.

"Uh, I'm uh—"

She stepped forward so she nearly touched the man, glowering at him all the while. But instead of being intimidated, the disheveled man let out a little huff of laughter and ran a hand over his face. "So the jig is up, huh?" he said in a thick Jersey accent.

He was *laughing* at her. How dare he? He'd invaded her life, her workplace, and followed her like a stalker, and he had the audacity to mock her? Lucia's nostrils flared as she sucked in a deep, fortifying breath and clenched her hands to stop them from trembling. She was so mad she thought she might cry but it was Grandpa she wanted to throttle. This man wasn't worth her anger. She wouldn't give this loser the satisfaction.

She made a show of unfurling her arms and tilting up her chin so she could look him square in the eye. Really she was struggling to think of the words she needed to put this man in his place—her English fluency had grown exponentially during the last six weeks but wildly out of control emotions had a tendency to frazzle the section of her brain that could translate.

The man seemed to note the change in her demeanor though and he threw his hands up. "Look, I'm not looking for any trouble. I'm just getting paid to keep an eye on you. Bring you home when you come to your senses."

Bring you back home? Who did this guy think he was? She was a grown woman. She didn't need a babysitter and she certainly didn't need some stranger threatening to send her back to Italy.

"Unless you want a harassment lawsuit and a restraining order under your name, I'd suggest you leave this restaurant and tell my grandfather that you're quitting."

He continued to study her while popping a handful of bar nuts into his mouth. His jaw moved as he chewed but still he didn't talk. At first she thought the man hadn't heard her.

Lucia opened her mouth to continue her tirade when he spoke. "Who's your grandfather?"

Chapter 4

Ryan couldn't tear his eyes away from the mini storm that was brewing at the end of the bar between Lucia and the shady guy who'd been leering at her from the moment he walked in. Ryan had assumed it was another admirer—Lucia had already acquired a small army of devoted male fans at the bar in her three days as an employee.

But then she'd gone up to this guy and confronted him. As if she knew him.

He wished he could hear what they were saying but all could do was watch Lucia's expression. With every new emotion he saw there, Ryan battled the urge to jump over the bar and slam his fist into the guy's face.

She was upset, that much was certain. But why?

Maybe he should intervene. But what if this guy was her ex or something?

"Whoa, dude, watch it." Javier stepped back, just missing the dirty dishrag Ryan chucked in his direction. Javier pointed to the concoction Ryan had been mixing. "What are you making there, some new-fangled non-alcoholic drink?"

Ryan looked down to see that he had been pouring simple syrup into the glass instead of vodka.

Javier laughed as Ryan let out a muffled curse before slinging the contents of the glass into the sink.

He pulled out a fresh glass and the requisite bottle of vodka but he couldn't resist sneaking glances at Lucia and the stranger. "Any idea what's going on over there?"

Now it was Javier's turn to curse and Ryan looked over in surprise. "What is it? Do you know that guy?"

Javier shook his head, irritation written all over him. "I told her to stay away from him. That girl is *loco*."

"Who is it?" When Javier didn't answer immediately, Ryan grabbed his arm. "Jav, who is this guy?"

Javier swatted his hand away. "She says he's INS, man."

Ryan looked from Javier to the non-descript man at the end of the bar. Yeah, he could see that. But why would immigration officials care so much about Lucia?

As if reading his thoughts, Javier said, "Wonder how she got on their radar. The poor girl is just trying to wait some tables—badly, sure, but that shouldn't be a crime."

Ryan was too busy watching the interaction in front of him to pay much attention to Javier. Why would the feds have it in for her? He took one look at the shock and fear on Lucia's face and the 'why' no longer mattered. All that mattered was that he put a stop to this while he still could.

"Watch the bar for me," he said to Javier as he pushed his friend out of his way and headed toward Lucia. Javier tried to stop him. "It's not your business, dude." But Ryan kept walking until he reached them.

Their conversation came to an abrupt halt when he showed up at their side and placed a possessive arm around Lucia's shoulders. She turned her face up to him in surprise and he gave her shoulders a little squeeze. Her eyes widened in surprise but before she could say anything, he turned to the man.

"Is there a problem here?"

The stranger eyed him with a disconcerting look of amusement. "Who are you? The boyfriend?"

Ryan's heart rate sped up and the muscle in his jaw clenched at the man's dismissive, condescending tone. Who did this guy think he was?

Lucia turned to him and gently pushed against his chest. "It's okay, I've got this."

He may have believed her—he may have even walked away to let her handle her business on her own—if he hadn't seen the fear in her eyes. There was no way in hell he'd leave her to deal with this goon on her own.

Ryan turned back to the man. "The question is, who are *you*? And what are you doing at my bar?"

The guy's face lit up with a mocking smile. "Oh, so this is your bar, huh?"

Ryan's hands clenched and unclenched at his side. Damn right this was his bar. And Lucia was his employee and his....well, not his girl. But she was his friend. Kinda. A wave of possessiveness swept over him. Whatever her role in his life, he needed to keep her safe.

The stranger looked back and forth between Lucia and Ryan, his eyes narrowed as though trying to figure out a puzzle. While looking straight at Lucia, he addressed his next comment to Ryan. "The people I work for say your friend here shouldn't be working here. She doesn't belong in this country. Isn't that right, Lucia?"

Ryan could feel Lucia stiffen beneath his arm.

She didn't belong here? So he knew she was here illegally. If so, he was taking his sweet time doing anything about it and seemed content to stand here and torture this girl. He was practically taunting her. There was a chance he could still put an end to this. For now, at least. It may not help her in the long run but it would wipe that smirk off of this jerk's face.

Before he could think it through, Ryan opened his mouth. "My wife belongs here, with me."

Lucia's gasp was quiet enough that only he heard and for a split second the look of shock on the stranger's face was all that mattered.

But then all three were startled by the sound of a low voice that was cold as ice.

"You two are married?"

Lucia and Ryan spun around to face the owner of the dark, ominous voice.

Oh crap. Daniel Gladwell. The man Ryan had spent the last four months trying to get close to and the past decade despising from a distance. And now here he was, less than six inches from his face and.... he was glowering. No, *glaring*. His eyes were practically boring holes into Ryan's skull.

The stranger was still behind them, listening to every word so Ryan glanced at Lucia, who looked just as shocked by Daniel's sudden appearance. "Uh, yes?" he said.

"*Oh merda,*" Lucia whispered, just loud enough that Ryan heard it.

Daniel's heavy stare shifted from Ryan to Lucia. His brows lifted with a look of mild curiosity, and the heat in his stare lessened considerably. He looked almost....kind. "Lucia?" he asked. "Care to explain?"

Wait a second. How did Daniel know Lucia's name?

"Danny, it's not what you think," Lucia said.

Danny? *Danny*?! The cold, hard man standing in front of them with his perfect suits and his flawless appearance and stiff posture....this was not a Danny. Mr. Gladwell, sure. Maybe Daniel to his family. But *Danny*?

Daniel stared at them, his face unreadable, but then his eye was caught by the stranger behind them. With a quick glance over his shoulder Ryan could see the man's look of awe as he took in the mighty tycoon who was addressing them like he was the emperor of Rome and not just the hotel's owner.

"Who are you?" Daniel asked, his jaw clenched and his expression hardened to a grim mask.

The man, who had been smirking and gloating moments before, turned into a bumbling buffoon in the face of Daniel's irritation.

"I, uh, I'm here because, uh…that is to say—"

Lucia's nose crinkled up before she spun back toward Daniel. "Marco hired him."

Marco? Who the hell was Marco? She didn't explain. "Marco hired him" was all she said, but Daniel's expression shifted from annoyance to surprise to outright anger. Turning his head to make a low comment to the bodyguard at his side, he turned back to the man in question. "These men will escort you to my office."

The stranger was whisked away by the burly guards and then it was just the three of them—a cozy group made up of Lucia, Daniel, and Ryan. Maybe now he could figure out how Daniel knew who Lucia was and why someone named Marco had sent someone to harass her.

But the moment they were left alone, Lucia and Daniel turned to face one another and started speaking in rapid-fire Italian, with only a few words recognizable to Ryan, whose main interaction with the Italian language included pasta names and wine varietals. He thought he caught the word "famiglia" and maybe "tu madre" before they seemed to remember his existence. First it was Lucia, who stopped speaking mid-sentence and turned to look at him.

He wished he knew what he saw in those eyes. They were filled with emotion but he couldn't put his finger on what.

What the hell was going on? Her lips were clamped shut—clearly in no hurry to explain. What was he missing here? Who was the stranger that Marco had hired? Who was Marco? How did she know Daniel so well? So many questions he didn't know where to begin.

At her silence, Daniel's speech seemed to come to an end as well and soon both were staring at him like he was a stranger from a strange land.

Ryan needed to say something. Anything. But he was so out of his depth, he couldn't begin to formulate a sentence. Daniel almost came to his rescue when he said a few Italian words in a low voice and Lucia went hurrying off toward the back hallway, which led to the managers' offices. But not before she shot him a look that said "I'm sorry."

"So you and Lucia are married?" Daniel's voice was even but Ryan could have sworn he was laughing at him.

"Uh, well…." Ryan scratched the back of his neck, looking for any way out of this mess. He'd wanted to gain Daniel's attention, but not like this. Not because he was lying about being married to someone Daniel clearly knew. *How?* Again, the question of how Lucia knew Daniel so well nagged at him, begging to be answered.

Daniel shoved his hands in his pockets and rocked back on his heels, studying Ryan like he was a piece of art hanging in a gallery. "Why did you do it?"

That question made his brain go completely blank. What did Daniel want to hear? This was his chance to speak to the devil himself. If he didn't play this right he could ruin his plan and, more importantly, he could screw things up for Lucia. "Um, I, uh…"

Daniel raised one brow and his amusement was obvious. "She certainly isn't into you for your wit, is she?"

That was it. Ryan shook off the initial shock of seeing his infamous nemesis up close. This was what he was here for—to meet this man, talk to him, earn his trust. His brother would be furious if he could see him now, finally face to face with the man, the myth, the legend, and he couldn't think of a single thing to say.

He cleared his throat and met Daniel's mocking gaze. "Lucia is a sweet girl, Mr. Gladwell. I didn't want to see her get into trouble."

Some of the mockery seemed to fade from Daniel's expression. Instead, he seemed to be sizing him up. "How very noble of you, Mr. ….."

"Smith. Ryan Smith." The fake name slipped off his tongue with ease. For one brief moment he wondered how Daniel would react if he'd used his real name. He shook off that thought. What had he called him. Noble? "It wasn't noble, sir. I'm the one who hired Lucia, if there's any trouble it shouldn't come down on her."

Daniel's expression was unreadable. "Come with me."

It wasn't a question, it was an order. Ryan glanced over to Javier who was watching their interaction with unabashed interest. Javier had no idea why he was really working at the bar but he knew how rare it was for anyone to get face time with the high and mighty hotel owner.

He saw his friend mouth, "Ask for a raise" before he turned to follow the quiet, intimidating tycoon into the back hallways that led to the general manager's office.

Shutting the door behind them, Daniel sat behind the desk and gestured to Ryan to take the empty seat across from him. "How long have you been working here, Ryan?"

"A few months."

"Do you like your job?" Daniel asked.

Ryan nodded. He could only half pay attention since the rest of his brain was replaying the little interaction he'd witnessed between Daniel and Lucia. Who was she to him? How did they know one another and, if they were so close, why did he seem shocked to find her there?

"Look," Daniel said, leaning over to rest his elbows on the desk. "I'll be honest with you...."

Daniel Gladwell was going to be honest for once? This should be good. *I screwed over your father and ruined your family.*

Bitter laughter threatened to erupt at the thought of Daniel actually coming clean. What would his brother do if this man owned up to his actions and—heaven forbid—actually apologized for his part in their father's downfall?

"Lucia is important to me. I appreciate what you did for her tonight," Daniel said, his voice surprisingly soft.

What had he done? Lied for her?

"We're, uh...we're not really married, sir."

Daniel actually laughed then and the sound was unnervingly....human. Not at all in keeping with the soulless android image he'd projected from a distance.

"Yeah, Lucia told me. Probably for the best, you wouldn't survive a day at the villa."

Before he could question Daniel's sanity or ask what the hell "the villa" was, Daniel continued. "As you may have gathered, Lucia is no stranger to me. She's...." Daniel seemed at a loss for words which was almost as alarming as his laughter. "She's family," he finally said.

Family? Lucia Jones was a member of Daniel's *family?*

Ryan found himself gaping at Daniel. "She never said. I mean... she only said she needed a job."

Daniel shook his head in seeming disbelief. "She said that, huh?"

"Isn't it true?" Ryan shifted in his seat, uncomfortable at the idea that Lucia had been lying to him all along. He thought back to the sad look on her face when she'd come in for the job.

Daniel ignored his question. "I'll deal with Lucia, don't worry about her. I just wanted to say thank you. I know you thought you were helping her back there."

Ryan looked up and found Daniel fixing him with a serious stare. "You were there for my family when it mattered. I won't forget that," Daniel said.

What the hell was he supposed to say to that?

"Yeah, well," Ryan said, standing from the chair and wiping his sweaty palms on his work pants. "No problem."

He left the office half expecting the soundtrack from *The Godfather* to be playing in the hallway. Had he seriously been summoned to Daniel Gladwell's office for a pat on the back?

Ryan froze halfway between the office and the bar. Had he really just sat there and said, "No problem?" He groaned aloud at the memory. What was he going to tell Billy? This had been his chance—his one opportunity to talk to the devil himself.

One of the reasons Ryan had been selected to be the mole was because of his ability to get along with just about anybody. Their dad used to call him the snake charmer as a kid because he was so good at sweet-talking his way out of any situation.

Billy had convinced him that this would be no different. All he had to do was wait for the perfect moment. He'd never doubted that once he got his foot in the door it would be smooth sailing. He hadn't over-thought what he would say or how he would say it; he'd merely trusted himself to be able to manipulate whatever situation he was in.

He leaned against the hallway wall and let his head drop back with a thud. That had been his chance. His big opportunity to work his magic and sweet-talk his way into Gladwell's inner circle. And he'd blown it. He hadn't been able to get his mind off of Lucia and the lies she'd told. A bitter taste filled his mouth at the realization that he'd been duped; she'd played him for a fool, lying to him from day one.

More than that, he couldn't stop thinking about the insinuations Daniel had made and his comments about her. It couldn't be true. There was no way the clumsy hottie at his bar could be related to the devil who'd ruined his family. Her sweetness, the humble way she'd thrown herself into serving…why would she do that if she came from money? No, there was no way his angel could be related to the devil.

Chapter 5

Lucia threw her purse down with a thud. *How dare he*? Marco had ruined everything. Who did he think he was hiring someone to look out for her? What was it the investigator had said? "To bring you home when you came to your senses."

This was exactly why she'd left him in the first place. He treated her like a child rather than her own woman. They were the same age but he always seemed to think he knew what was best for her. He treated her dreams like they were silly fairytales and outright laughed at her plans. To think, she'd dated him for more than a decade without seeing him for who he really was. She'd been so content being his perfect girlfriend. Self-loathing made her stomach churn. How humiliating that she'd spent so many years without seeing the truth. And even now, after all these months away, he was still treating her like a child.

Lucia fell onto the bed face first with a muffled groan. At least she'd eventually come to her senses. Better late than never. And it was all thanks to Daniel. Well, Daniel and Ivy. When they showed up at the villa as her grandfather's guests—for the first time in her life she'd witnessed real love. It had been eye-opening to compare what she had with Marco to their fiery, all-consuming chemistry. But she'd ignored the twinge of doubts, telling herself that what she and her then-fiancé had was more realistic, more…comfortable.

And maybe she could have kept telling herself that but then, after yet another fight with Marco about her dreams to pursue fashion rather than follow in her grandfather's footsteps, she'd escaped for a fun little weekend getaway to Paris. With Jack and Holly.

Watching the two of them fall in love had been the last straw. More than that, she saw the way they complemented each other and believed in one another. That was when she knew that she couldn't hide from the truth any longer—what she and Marco had wasn't built to last. She had been settling.

She may not be a romantic like her grandfather, but she did believe in love and when she married, she would settle for nothing less than the real deal. But that wasn't happening anytime soon. She had other dreams that came first. Her career was her first and only priority. One would think her tycoon of a grandfather would understand that, but no. All he cared about was marrying off his children and grandchildren and playing matchmaker for everyone around him. Just look at poor Daniel and Jack. They hadn't stood a chance once her grandpa got involved.

Lucia rolled over and stared at the ceiling. She missed Gretchen now more than ever—her constant chatter would have been the perfect distraction. Even better, she wished Holly or Ivy were here, at least then she would have someone to talk to about everything that had happened—the private detective who'd followed her, the way Ryan had tried to save her, and Daniel's comical look of shock when he'd shown up at the exact wrong time.

Her laughter sounded loud in the empty apartment and she found herself clapping a hand over her mouth to smother the sound. It wasn't funny, Daniel could ruin everything.

But he wouldn't. She knew her friend well enough to know that he wouldn't force her to go home. He wouldn't fire her if she explained how important it was that she be able to stand on her own two feet.

But Ryan might.

That thought brought an abrupt end to the laughter. Her anger and humiliation was instantly replaced by a crushing guilt. She was haunted by the look on Ryan's face when Daniel had arrived. She'd seen the surprise and confusion when she and Daniel had started talking in Italian and then, when she'd walked away, she could have sworn he'd looked hurt. And she couldn't blame him—she'd caused nothing but trouble for him with her lies.

How could she face Ryan?

He was kind enough to give her a job and show her the ropes and how did she repay him? By lying. Everything he knew about her was a lie. Her heart ached at the memory of Ryan standing up for her, protecting her. The guy had been willing to pretend to be her husband, for heaven's sake, and she hadn't even been honest about her name.

Or the fact that she was an heiress.

Lucia closed her eyes and groaned. What would he think when he found out the truth? This man who'd given up everything so he could make enough money to save his family. She could vividly remember the disdain in his voice when he'd talked about how glad he was that he hadn't been raised with money. What was it he'd said? *Better to grow up learning how to manage in the real world than be a spoiled rich kid with nothing but dreams.* Those words still stung even though he hadn't been talking about her at the time. But he might as well have been. That was almost exactly how Marco had described her. He'd called her entitled, spoiled, told her she was living in a fantasy. Maybe he'd been right all along. She really *was* a spoiled rich kid with nothing but dreams.

There's no way Ryan would let her keep her job. And why should he? There were plenty of people out there who really needed that job. She could practically hear his voice saying those words. And a part of her agreed with him. He would never understand why she'd done what she did.

Her eyes shot open. But then again….maybe he would.

Lucia popped up in bed, her heart pumping as though she'd run up a flight of stairs. Maybe he *would* understand—well, maybe not the spoiled heiress part—but he knew all about familial obligations and needing money. That was one thing they had in common. And maybe she could use that to her advantage.

Puzzle pieces were falling into place in Lucia's brain. How had she not thought of it before?

The only thing standing in the way of her and her trust fund was six long years…or marriage. And who said the marriage had to be real? Or for love? People married for reasons other than love all the time. Why not her? After all it was an archaic loophole keeping her from the money that would one day be hers. Why not exploit it?

She was breathless with excitement. Or was it fear? But there was no danger, not as long as she found a husband who understood the rules and was in it for the same reason. For money. As long as she and her partner in crime agreed ahead of time to annul the marriage, she could have her career and one day, when she met the man of her dreams, she could still have her dream marriage. It was so simple.

All that was standing in the way of her and her dreams was the lack of a husband. And all that was standing in the way of Ryan and his goal of saving his family was a lack of money. They could help each other and get everything they dreamed of.

Excitement had adrenaline coursing through her system and Lucia hopped out of bed. Just thinking of the possibilities her trust fund would give her was exhilarating. Once she'd called off the wedding with Marco she'd been certain her only option was to make money on her own or wait until she turned thirty but now....she could have it all.

If Ryan agreed. He was the obvious choice—she trusted him. Plus, he needed money too. It was a win-win.

Her excitement took a momentary leave of absence and was replaced by cold trepidation. What if he said no? After all, why would he help her, the woman who'd been lying to him? The woman who was the living definition of the rich brats he despised. If he said no, who else could she ask? It wasn't like she had a ton of friends in this city and the odds of finding someone she trusted to keep up their end of the bargain were slim. But Ryan...she could trust him. After his bold claim about being her husband tonight, he was practically her knight in shining armor. He would never take advantage of her. And she couldn't think of any other man she would trust with this. The only problem was, did he still trust her?

Flopping back down onto the bed, Lucia tried to form reasonable thoughts despite the fact that her heart was pounding and her hands were shaking, whether from excitement, nerves, or fear was yet to be determined.

She couldn't go through with this. What would her grandfather say? What would Marco say? Oh, who cared what Marco would say. His opinion no longer mattered. More importantly, what would Ryan say? She groaned aloud as a fleeting image of Ryan's disgust at the mere proposition flitted through her brain. He would think she was crazy. He'd think she was a money-hungry, spoiled brat with no work ethic.

And maybe he'd be right.

No. She had to forcibly remind herself of the many long hours and days and weeks and months she'd poured into her dream of being a designer. She had a fantastic work ethic...just not for her grandfather's work. She wanted to stand on her own two feet—she just needed a little help from her mother's trust fund. That wasn't a crime.

They could both benefit from this agreement. She just had to make him see that.

* * * *

Ryan gave a little salute to Javier, the last employee to head out for the night. As usual, Ryan was alone behind the bar, counting the till so he could close up for the night. The shiny bottles of whiskey lined up perfectly seemed to call to him out of the corner of his eye. A few shots were exactly what he needed to put this whole disastrous night behind him.

The bar had been busy, which was the perfect distraction. But even so, he'd managed to find time throughout the night to obsess over every word he'd overheard and every lie Lucia had told him.

No, not lies. It was what she hadn't told him that stung.

Could she really be related to Daniel? He'd said she was family, why would he lie about that? That thought was a slap in the face. Daniel must have known she was here. But if she was related to the owner, it made no sense that she was so desperate for money. Or why she'd lied about her name.

Ryan swallowed down his anger. He would probably never know her reasons; what mattered was she'd lied. He shook his head as he wiped down the bar one last time. His own hypocrisy was laughable. It wasn't like he'd told Lucia the real story of why he was working there. But still. He'd known Lucia was hiding something, that much had been obvious. And he wouldn't have cared all that much if her secret was....well, anything else. But the fact that she was related to the man who had single-handedly destroyed his family? That was hard to swallow.

Ryan looked down at the wad of cash in his hands and cursed. Dammit, he'd lost track again and would have to start from the top. He froze at the sound of the bar door opening. Dammit, Javier forgot to lock up on his way out. Experience told him it was either a hotel guest who was already two sheets to the wind and looking for one last nightcap or his brother, come to check in on his progress.

God, what was he going to tell his brother?

When the visitor didn't speak, Ryan glanced over his shoulder and froze.

Lucia stood in the doorway, her wide eyes glistening in the dark. She looked terrified. "Lucia? What are you doing here?"

His voice seemed to wake her from her spell and she moved toward him quickly, her lips pressed together, and her gaze unblinking. She looked like a woman on a mission. Ryan leaned over the bar with a sigh. Lucia had probably come to apologize, or explain, maybe. This should be good.

Lucia reached the bar and sat down on one of the stools, still bundled up in her jacket and her steely gaze never leaving his. Ryan didn't look away. He stared right back, waiting for the excuses to begin.

He watched her swallow and shift in her seat.

Here we go.

She inhaled deeply and he saw her hands tremble before she clasped them in her lap. "I think we should get married."

Time stood still as Ryan stared at Lucia. Disbelief had him frozen in place. Clearly she was joking. But her lips were set in a grim line as she waited for his response. She wasn't laughing. Which meant, she wasn't joking. The blood in his veins seemed to come to a halt. The silence turned deafening and the only movement was Lucia's subtle but telling nervous movements as she reached out to toy with the edge of the bar rag sitting in front of her.

"It's funny," Ryan finally said. "I thought you said, 'We should get married.'"

Lucia frowned at his response. "I did." She leaned over the bar. "Let me explain."

Ryan struggled not to laugh out loud. He couldn't help it—this was ridiculous and this feisty little Italian was really cute when she was acting insane. But this was no joke, Lucia was talking about marriage—the word alone felt like a weight on his shoulders. He'd seen what marriage had done to his parents and it was one of many institutions not meant for him. But hell, he couldn't wait to her this.

Lucia launched into her explanation with clipped tones. "I'm an heiress. My family has a lot of money. A lot. But they didn't support my dreams of being a fashion designer so I came here to make it on my own."

She paused to take a breath and Ryan realized his mouth was hanging open. She was an heiress. Did those even exist in real life? Before his stunned brain could even begin to process, she continued.

"But, you see, I ran out of money and that's why I needed this job. I didn't want to go home a failure like my—well, I didn't want to do that. I have pride."

His eyes followed as she licked her lips before continuing on, leaning over the bar even further so she was nearly touching him. "But the thing is, I have money but I can't access it until I turn thirty or get married. Which is where you come in. I need money, you need money. If you marry me, we can both have our money."

She looked up at him, her brows raised and her eyes full of hope. "So?" she asked. "What do you think?"

Ryan repeated the words that kept echoing in his skull. "You're an heiress."

"Yes."

"To a fortune."

She rolled her eyes. "Yes."

Well, color him unperceptive. How had Billy and Javier both guessed that she was rich and he'd been a blind fool? She had yet to explain how she was related to Daniel Gladwell but if she was an heiress and they were related, that must mean Daniel came from serious money too. And here he'd bought all those stories in the press about Daniel being a self-made man. He really was naïve.

Lucia reached out a hand and placed it on top of his.

The simple touch set his body on fire and Ryan's mind chose that moment to become a muddled mess. Dammit, he couldn't think straight when she was this close. Her eyes were locked with his and all he could find himself thinking about was how beautiful her eyes were—the color of dark chocolate, with a depth that made him feel like she could see right through him. There were far more pressing matters to be considering but there it was. He was fascinated. They were captivating.

She was lovely, there was no doubt about it. From her soft voice with its Italian accent, to the long wavy black hair and doe eyes, the woman before him was compelling in every way. Sweet and stubborn, she was ridiculously fun to tease. She was perfection—like everything about her had been created just for him. That thought sent a chill down his spine. He couldn't be thinking of relationships and romantic emotions, not when his family was such a mess and he had a revenge plan to enact before he could finally be free to start a life. But like it or not, this girl sitting before him—she was his perfect woman.

And she'd just proposed.

"Ryan," she prodded. "What do you think?"

Ryan pushed himself back from the bar. "I think that might be the least romantic proposal I've ever heard."

Lucia sighed and tossed the bar rag at him. "I'm serious."

And she was. From the way she was sitting and the hard tone, there was no denying she was serious. But she clearly wasn't in her right mind. No sane person married a relative stranger so they could access their trust fund. It didn't happen—at least not outside of the movies. The whole idea was crazy.

Ryan leaned over the bar again, and this time he was the one who stared her down. It was time for some reason. "Look, I'm flattered, I really am," he started.

She rolled her eyes again but didn't interrupt.

"But I don't think you've thought this through."

Lucia's eyes narrowed at that. "Don't be condescending."

"I'm not!" Ryan held his hands up in defense. "I swear, I'm not. I just don't think you've thought of all your options. I mean, there have to be better ways to make money."

Lucia let out a little laugh at that and Ryan tried not to be distracted by the sound or the direct correlation her laugh had on his groin.

"Tell me, oh wise one, what other options can you come up with to make millions overnight?"

The word "millions" seemed to hang in the air. Ryan opened his mouth to speak but couldn't think of a response. *Millions overnight* was still playing on a loop in his brain.

Apparently Lucia sensed his hesitation because she leapt up from her seat, shedding her coat, all the while watching him with wide, questioning eyes.

"Look, Lucia—" The words died in his throat as he took in the sight before him. Lucia was standing there clad in a flimsy slip of a camisole and figure-hugging leggings of some sort and the sight left him speechless.

She was stunning from the tanned smooth skin of her shoulders to the rounded hips. Forcing his eyes back up, he willed himself not to look at her body, but that did little to help. She was staring at him in concern now, her brows pulled together to create a cute little crease above her nose and those lips....they were pouting at him in a way that was positively, unintentionally suggestive.

He spun around so he was facing the till once more, his back to Lucia and his erection safely hidden from view. Taking a long deep breath, he ordered himself to get a grip. This woman was sexy and feisty, but she was also young and naive...and she'd just proposed marriage. Now was not the time to turn into a teen going through puberty.

"Are you okay?" Lucia was right next to him behind the bar. Her scent washed over him and he was powerless, completely wrecked.

"Yeah, fine," he managed. She took a step toward him and he found himself inching back as though she was a tiger and not a five-foot-nothing slip of a girl....who just happened to be talking crazy at the moment.

Shoving a hand through his hair to keep from reaching out for her, he let out a sigh. "This is nuts. We can't get married."

She put her palms on her hips, which thrust her chest out further, making the flimsy camisole strain against her breasts, causing his erection to strain against his pants.

"Why?" she demanded. "Why can't we?"

The sexual frustration made his voice gruffer than he intended. "Because I don't even know who you are."

Lucia flinched and her arms dropped to her sides as an awkward silence fell between them.

All of the frustration he'd been feeling since the moment he'd realized she'd been lying to him and that she was somehow related to Daniel, came bubbling up to the surface. "Seriously, Lucia, who are you? Clearly you're not the down-on-her-luck poor girl you claimed to be."

"I never claimed that," she mumbled. She was looking down at her feet now as though the answer could be found in the bar mat beneath her.

He was being a hypocrite and he knew it….and he didn't care. He may not have been upfront about his motives for being behind the bar but he had opened up to her—about his family, and his father. Something he rarely did. No, something he *never* did.

And it wasn't just any secret she'd been hiding. She was related to Daniel Gladwell, the man who'd ruined his family's life and the man he was hell bent on exposing. He could hear his brother's voice whispering in his ear. This was his chance. Lucia was his ticket to get to Daniel. Daniel had spelled it out clear as day. This girl standing before him was a weakness, a chink in Daniel's otherwise steel-clad armor.

No. He pushed that thought aside. Lucia had nothing to do with his family's problems or his plans to get even. But still, the connection couldn't be denied.

"Daniel said you were related," he said. He watched Lucia shift uncomfortably before him and tried not to stare at the skimpy lace string that threatened to slip off her shoulder. "How are you related?" he pushed.

Lucia looked up at him then and the guilt in her eyes was nearly his undoing. She looked so sad and apologetic he almost backtracked and told her to forget it, to keep her secrets.

"He said that?" Before he could ask anything more, she took another step toward him so they were almost touching and shook her head like she was brushing off the question. "It doesn't matter. That's not important."

Not important? He nearly laughed aloud at that.

"What matters is that we both have the same need, the same wants," she pushed on.

She was looking up at him with hypnotic eyes and her lips were slightly parted and….holy hell, he'd completely lost track of what they were talking about.

"The same needs?" he echoed stupidly. She couldn't be talking about sex…could she? Did she feel it too, this physical connection….the electricity between them that—

"Money," she said.

The word was cold water in his face and it brought him back to reality with a jolt.

Money. Right. Of course it was about money. She was related to Gladwell, after all.

"Why can't you ask your family for the money?"

Lucia's lips clamped shut.

"Seriously, why can't you ask them for a loan at the very least. If you've got millions tucked away in a trust fund, your family is obviously loaded."

"They wouldn't give it to me." Lucia chewed on her lip before she added, "Besides, I need to do this on my own."

Ryan laughed in disbelief. "Right, doing it on your own...aside from using your family's money."

Lucia's brows drew together in a scowl.

So she was getting annoyed. Good. "How are you related to Daniel?" he asked again.

"I don't want to talk about Daniel, and I don't want to talk about my family." Her chest rose as she drew in a deep breath. "Will you marry me or not?"

The fact that she yelled the actual proposal might have been funny if he wasn't so on edge, bristling with anger and a frustration that ran so deep he could barely see straight.

She moved even closer so mere inches separated them and she rested one hand against his chest. Those soulful eyes were staring up at him. "Please, just think about it."

That little bit of contact broke his resolve. Closing the distance between them, he wrapped an arm around her waist, pulling her up against him and crushed her lips with his own.

The contact was so electric, so hot, he heard a little moan escape Lucia before she wrapped her arms around his neck and kissed him back with a passion he'd never experienced.

Lucia tilted her head back giving him more access and he took advantage, his tongue claiming her mouth. The kiss was blinding in its heat. The world slipped away as he held her close, reveling in the feel of her breasts pressed against his chest, her warm skin beneath his hands, her soft lips moving against his, matching the urgency that was nearly overwhelming.

He moved her so she was perched on the ice machine and she wrapped her legs around his hips, holding him close, pressing against him with a little whimper that was unbearably sexy. He moved one hand around to cup her breast, which was straining against the material. She moaned and her head fell back, exposing her neck. He trailed kisses along her neck, her shoulder, and his thumb flicked over her hard nipple.

God, he wanted this, he wanted *her*. Here. Now.

The ice machine chose that moment to make a loud, tumbling sound, jarring Ryan back to his senses. He froze. 'Here and now' was behind a bar. And not just any bar, it was the bar where he worked. For Daniel. Who was somehow related to this woman in his arms.

Ryan pulled back, though moving away from her was like defying gravity. Her eyes were hazy with passion as he gently disentangled her arms from around his neck.

He watched her fall back to earth and the lust and passion that had left her flushed and dazed was quickly replaced by an embarrassed awkwardness as she tried to shift away from him and straighten her clothes. Moving back so she could hop off of the ice machine, he shoved his hands in his pockets to keep from reaching for her again.

What was wrong with him? This woman was the last person on earth he should be getting entangled with. She was related to the devil himself. She was on the other side of huge divide and if she was anything like Daniel, she would be as ruthless and cold as the great tycoon who'd destroyed his father and his family without a second thought. If she was anything like Gladwell, it would always just be about money for her.

As if to prove his point, she spoke up then, her voice was breathier than usual but that was the only giveaway that she was rattled by their kiss. "Think about my offer, Ryan. This could be your opportunity to help your family—"

Hearing her mention family stoked the fire of an anger that had been a part of his life for longer than he could remember. She knew nothing of his family or their problems. How could she? She was a self-described heiress. There's no way she could fathom what it was like to go from wealth to poverty overnight—to give up your dreams to help your family get what they rightfully deserved. Worse, she was related to the very man who'd destroyed his family. How dare she claim to have sympathy, when it was her relatives who'd taken advantage and left them to rot?

His next words came out through gritted teeth. "You don't know anything about my family."

Lucia stared at him for a moment, clearly taken aback by his sharp tone. "Fine. But I know that you need money as much as I do."

Ryan shook his head. "I need money. You *want* it. There's a difference, but I wouldn't expect a spoiled brat to understand that."

Even Ryan was shocked by the harshness of his words but he couldn't bring himself to take it back. Because it was true. He may not know her circumstances but she clearly came from wealth and had the world at her fingertips. It was only her pride in the way....and impatience. It was people like her—like her family, rather—who took what they had for granted and pay no heed to the consequences of their actions.

Lucia's face was flushed and he saw her chest rise and fall rapidly. For one terrifying moment he thought she was going to cry but instead she turned on her heel and marched back the way she'd come, pausing only long enough to call over her shoulder, "Screw you, Ryan."

Chapter 6

Lucia would have loved nothing more than to wallow in bed after a sleepless night but now that her secret was out, Ivy and Daniel had insisted she stop by for breakfast. Daniel left for work shortly after they'd eaten, leaving Lucia and Ivy to lounge on the hotel suite's overstuffed couches as they took turns entertaining Baby Anna.

"It was a disaster," Lucia said for the millionth time. She'd told Ivy everything—well, almost everything—about her fight with Ryan the night before. She'd left out the part where she'd proposed. She wasn't quite ready to hear anyone else's lectures on that particular topic. Not yet, at least. Ivy had listened without interrupting but once she was done, Ivy handed her the baby and picked up her phone to call her sister, Holly.

"She needs to weigh in on this," Ivy said. "No one has more experience with mysterious bartenders than Holly."

Lucia conceded with a sigh as she gently pried her hair from Anna's fist.

"....so then Lucia went to the bar last night to apologize—" Ivy was saying.

"Ooh, romantic," Holly interrupted.

"Right. So romantic. *But* the hot bartender was not having it and they got into a fight."

Lucia listened as Ivy summed up her story, minus one very important little fact that she wasn't willing to share just yet.

"I need more details!" Holly's voice came from the phone on the coffee table.

Here's a little detail I may have left out. I proposed. Lucia trusted these two women with her life but she wasn't ready to explain her impulsive and, possibly borderline insane, proposal the night before. Besides, it didn't matter anymore. He'd said no.

Lucia winced at the memory. The rejection was disappointing but that wasn't what really stung. It was the look of revulsion on his face when it had sunk in that she was wealthy. Heck, she was way more than just "wealthy." She was heir to a dynasty. But considering how disgusted he'd seemed to be when he thought she was related to Daniel, it was probably best she'd kept her true family connections to herself. Daniel was successful, but her grandfather and their family business were in a whole other stratosphere of affluence. If he thought being related to Daniel was bad, he'd despise her if he found out her true background.

She looked up from the baby to see that Ivy was waiting for her to speak. Right, they were waiting to hear some juicy details. Lucia sighed. "Here's a detail. Ryan is a condescending, irritating jerk." That much was true. Every time she thought of his last words to her, she wanted to punch him in the face. But a nagging voice in the back of her brain was mocking her. Why had his words hurt so badly? *Because they were true.* She *was* a spoiled brat.

"And then she kissed him," Ivy called out to the speakerphone, interrupting Lucia's self-pitying thoughts.

"Oooh, this just got good." They heard some crunching on the other end of the line and Lucia would bet money that her friend was munching on popcorn as she listened—like Lucia's life was an episode of a *telenovela*.

At least her disastrous life was amusing to her friends.

"What are you going to do now?" Holly asked.

That was the question Lucia was still debating. What on earth would she do now? She swallowed the lump in her throat. Now she had no options. It wasn't like she could approach a complete stranger and ask him to marry her for her money. She'd spent her whole life trying to avoid gold-diggers, did she really want to go seeking one out? She let her head drop back against the couch. That was why Ryan had been so perfect. A bitter laugh escaped her as she realized that his disdain for her wealth was exactly what made him such an ideal choice. But no, apparently his disgust with her trumped his desire for money. She tried to figure out what she should do next but her options were depressing. She could go back to Italy with her tail between her legs like her mother had done. Her heart sank at the thought. Not only would she be following in her mother's miserable footsteps but she'd be giving Marco and her grandfather the satisfaction of admitting she'd failed. She couldn't do it, she just couldn't.

Lucia shrugged and tried to hold back the tears that were threatening to spill. Ivy moved to her side and wrapped an arm around her.

"If this is about money…" Ivy started.

The fact that Lucia had been waiting tables for money rather than letting her friends help her had not gone over well at breakfast. At all.

Particularly with Daniel. And now it seemed that Ivy was going to take up the cause.

Lucia waved her away and swiped at a tear. "I can't take your money." Pride had her lifting her chin resolutely. "But thanks," she added with a smile.

Ivy clamped her mouth shut and Lucia could all but see her fighting an inner battle. She relented with a nod. "Okay, but if you need anything—"

"You'll be the first person I go to," Lucia promised.

When Ivy continued to study her with concern, she added with all honesty, "It's not just about the job or the money...."

"You like him." Holly sounded like a judge handing down a verdict. She sounded so serious, Lucia almost laughed. Almost. She was too stunned to make a sound.

She turned to see Ivy nodding, her eyes filled with a motherly concern that was her undoing. She couldn't lie, not even to herself. Her reaction to his words and his judgment....she cared what he thought. And why wouldn't she? Aside from last night, he'd been nothing but kind to her. He made her laugh, and that kiss....good Lord, that kiss had done things to her she hadn't known were possible. That kiss had been sensational. Lucia muttered a curse under her breath. That kiss was amazing....and she wanted to do it again.

"I guess I do kind of like him. Even though he is a jerk."

Holly's sigh was so over the top, Lucia and Ivy both started to giggle.

"Crushes are the worst," Holly said.

"Oh yeah, they suck," Ivy added.

There was a moment of silence as Lucia digested these words of wisdom. She'd never felt this way before—needy and aching. If this was what it meant to have a crush, she wanted no part of them. Ivy was right, they did suck.

"But they're kinda great when they're reciprocated," Holly added.

Now it was Ivy's turn to let out a sappy sigh as she held out her arms for her daughter. "Yeah, they're pretty amazing."

Lucia rolled her eyes at her friends. It was easy for them to talk. They had their happily ever afters. Their crushes not only liked them back, they'd fallen head over heels. And Lucia? Well, hers looked at her like she'd grown a second head when he'd found out she came from money. A now-familiar stab of pain stole her breath as she remembered the sneer on his face when he'd called her a brat.

But then he'd kissed her.

And then he called her a spoiled brat. Talk about mixed messages.

Baby Anna was still on her lap and smiling up at her. The smile was contagious and Lucia gave the little girl a watery smile in return. "I don't know what do," Lucia admitted.

"What do you mean, you don't know what you're going to do?" Ivy said. "Don't you have a shift tonight?"

Lucia nodded. "But I can't go back there. Not with Ryan hating me. He thinks I'm some spoiled rich kid. And maybe he's right."

Holly's voice piped up in the middle of the room. "Coming from money doesn't make you spoiled, sweetie. You've been working since you were old enough to have a job—"

Lucia rolled her eyes. "Yeah, but at Grandpa's office."

"So?" Ivy said. "You still have a strong work ethic."

Lucia heaved a deep breath. "All of the money I came here with I made on my own."

"See?" Holly said. "Sounds like this Ryan guy has a chip on his shoulder that has absolutely nothing to do with you."

Ivy pulled back so she could face her. "Do you want to keep this job?"

"I *need* to keep this job," Lucia said with a pathetic laugh.

"Then why are you going to let this guy stop you?"

Ivy had a point and she knew it, but the idea of walking back into that restaurant and facing Ryan after everything that had happened the night before—the proposal, that kiss….his rejection. Another thought occurred to her. "What if he's told everyone I've been lying this whole time?"

"The only way to show them the real you is to go in there and be your sweet, charming, lovable self," Holly said. "And if they don't like you once they get to know you….they're not worth knowing."

Ivy was nodding in agreement so vehemently her auburn hair started slipping out of the topknot holding it off her face.

Lucia kept imagining what she would do or say if she went back to that bar tonight. What would Ryan say? What would she do? She was torn between slapping him for his rude rejection and begging him to let her explain. She dropped her head back against the couch with a sigh. Either way it involved her going back to the bar.

"Fine," she said. "I'll go."

* * * *

Ryan would have preferred to do pretty much anything else with his day off.

"Grab another box, you wuss." Billy shoved past him with his arms full of boxes.

His mother was already inside, putting away the kitchenware Ryan had just hauled inside the tiny studio apartment in Queens. He loaded up two more boxes and carried them inside.

His mother was already complaining—not that he was surprised. She'd done little else these last eight years, ever since his father had drunk himself into the grave. Things had gone from bad to worse to absolute hell and it all started when Daniel Gladwell stole the family company out from underneath their father. Years later they still suffered while Daniel sat up there in his cushy penthouse suite, with his beautiful wife and happy daughter.

And Lucia. Don't forget Lucia.

He'd known that Daniel had family in Italy. It was well known that he'd married his wife Ivy in Italy and stayed for months to be with family. If he'd been smart, he would have made the connection the first day he'd met Lucia. What were the odds that a random Italian chick happened to wander into Daniel Gladwell's bar? He'd been kicking himself for not seeing any of it sooner. The lies, the family connection, the wealthy background. He'd been blind to all of it.

He hadn't been blind to her. That had been the trouble from the start. He'd been blinded by her good looks and the way she laughed at herself and at him and that body and her eyes and the way her lips—

"What's wrong with you?" His mother stopped complaining long enough to turn her angry stare in his direction.

"Nothing's wrong, Ma."

His mother gave a sniff "Then why does it look like somebody just ran over your dog?"

"Again," Billy said with a snicker.

Ryan glared at his brother. "Seriously? Only a sick psychopath would find that funny. You loved that dog, too."

Billy dismissed him with a shrug as he started unpacking a box of electronics.

"That's the last of it," Ryan said, already inching toward the door. Surely by coming out to Queens and doing manual labor he had fulfilled his familial obligations for the day.

"Not so fast."

He turned to find his mother and brother watching him with matching grim looks. How had he never noticed the similarity before? Ryan had gotten his father's Irish features, with his dark hair and blue eyes, while Billy shared their mother's sandy blond hair and gray eyes. But it was more than just the physical similarity. At that moment, he saw the same negative tendencies, the ability to find fault with anyone and everyone around them. Particularly him.

And right now, he was clearly in the hot seat.

Resigning himself to the inevitable, he sank onto the couch which he and his brother had hauled minutes before. "All right, let's hear it. What did I do now?"

"You haven't done anything wrong, Ryan," his mother started.

"It's what you haven't done," Billy finished.

Seriously, did these two rehearse these scenes? Ryan rubbed his eyes and tried to explain. "I'm making progress, but it's not easy."

"What kind of progress?" His mother folded her arms as she waited for his response.

"Yeah, what have you been doing other than flirting with that new waitress?"

Ryan shifted on the couch. "Daniel called me into his office yesterday. He's taken a liking to me."

Well that wasn't *entirely* true…but it wasn't a lie either. It was a lie of omission.

Just like Lucia.

Dammit, why did all thoughts lead back to her? Ever since she'd stormed out of the bar last night, he hadn't been able to get her out of his mind. Guilt had him tossing and turning all night as his traitorous brain flashed an image of those hurt eyes staring up at him when he'd called her an entitled, spoiled brat.

Then this morning he'd obsessed over whether or not she would show up for her shift tonight. Clearly she didn't need the money…and it wasn't like she was a natural at it. She was probably halfway back to Italy by now, telling the rest of Daniel's family about the jerk of a bartender she'd kissed.

That kiss. The other reason he hadn't been able to get her off of his mind. That kiss had been earthshattering. Ryan had kissed his share of women before but none of those experiences could compare to the blazing fire she'd ignited.

"Yo, earth to Ryan." Billy was sneering at him and his mother did not look pleased.

Crap.

"Sorry, what?"

His mother spoke in slow motion, like he was hard of hearing. "What did that monster want?"

That monster. For as long as he could remember that was how she referred to Daniel. It had always seemed melodramatic to Ryan, but then that was his mother. She lived for drama. She'd raised her sons to think of Daniel as the boogeyman—some dark, twisted evil henchman who'd set out to ruin their lives. Ryan had outgrown the boogeyman stories ages ago and now, having met the man up close and personal, it was even harder to think of him as anything other than what he was—a man. Ruthless and heartless, perhaps, but just a man.

"He wanted to commend me on my quick thinking," Ryan said.

His brother scoffed and his mother scowled. "And how is that helping us? Huh?"

The two shared a knowing look that didn't bode well for him. Uh oh, here it comes.

"You're not there to make nice with the boss, you pansy," Billy said.

Ryan leaned back against the couch cushions. "Actually, that's exactly why I'm there, remember? To make nice and gain information. Watch his inner circle and keep my ear to the ground."

"And what have you learned so far?" his mother cut it. "Other than the fact that you're employee of the month."

He should be used to that derisive tone by now but even as an adult, her sharp tongue had the power to make him feel like a little kid who'd wet the bed. *I learned that Daniel has a mysterious relative working at the hotel who's on the run from someone.* It was tempting. They would latch onto this bit of news like leeches and before the day was over, he would be embroiled in some new farfetched revenge plot that somehow included Lucia. No. There was no way he could do that to her.

He watched his mother and brother, who were snapping at one another over whose stupid plan it had been to send him in in the first place.

"You didn't have any choice," he reminded them politely. "Billy the hothead over here isn't allowed within thirty yards of Daniel thanks to the fights he picked…with the *bellboy.*"

Billy's puffy face was pulled into a sneer. Not even he could argue that his attempt to get to Daniel had been a complete and utter whiskey-driven disaster.

"And Mother here couldn't do it since Daniel knows her so well from the takeover," he reminded them, as if this was a new fact. From the way his mother told the story, Daniel had blown through their company like a whirling dervish, destroying everything in his path. But not without some epic showdowns with his mother. Their father had never been the aggressive one in the family. That, he had left to their mother.

"That's right," she said. "It all comes down to you." It didn't take a mind reader or even a terribly intuitive person to see how disappointing that was to her. As if he was useless.

"I don't know what you want from me," Ryan said. "I'm keeping my ear to the ground like you asked. But seriously, what do you think I'm going to learn working behind a bar?"

Aside from the fact that he has a mysterious relative with a past. Who wanted to marry him. He shifted uncomfortably at that thought. He wasn't used to keeping secrets from his family, but Lucia was not a part of this. Liar or not, she didn't deserve to pay for Daniel's crimes.

"There have got to be some skeletons in that man's closet," his mother said. "Believe me, that man has his secrets. And we all know he has a weakness now...."

Oh no, not this again.

"That family of his will be his undoing, believe you me." His mother lit a cigarette and Ryan turned so he could open the window behind him for some non-toxic air.

"Mother, we are not going after an innocent woman and her baby. That's final."

His mother raised an eyebrow and peered at him over the smoking cigarette in her mouth. After she'd exhaled, she said, "Do you have a better plan? If not, I don't see any other option. We've been watching Gladwell for years....family is his only weakness."

Lucia is my family. Daniel's words echoed in his mind. Ivy and Baby Anna weren't the only family in Daniel's life. And he had access to this one.

"Have you forgotten what that man did to our family?" his brother asked. Billy had that motivational speaker look on his face. Before his brother could launch into a well-rehearsed diatribe on the evils of Daniel Gladwell, Ryan cut him off.

"I remember, okay? It's my family too. I remember the way the Gladwell takeover ruined Dad."

"That man left me with nothing," his mother added, never one to be left out of a pity party. Gesturing to the apartment around her she added. "Just look at how far we've fallen."

We. There she goes again. It was true that she'd lost everything when their father lost the business and then promptly passed away. But it wasn't like she'd done anything to help save them once they'd fallen. She and Billy had been content to sit back and scheme and plot vengeance rather than move forward or, heaven forbid, get a job. Which meant it had been up to him to work his way through school and attempt to start a new life. He'd been off to a pretty decent start with an entry-level job at a marketing company...before they'd managed to guilt-trip him into working at the bar.

He should be well on his way to a career by now but he had somehow gotten sucked back into their revenge plans. And for what?

His mother took another drag of her cigarette and answered his unspoken question. "He owes us." That was another one of her favorite refrains. *He owes us.* That's always what their revenge schemes came down to—the money they think they're owed.

"That's it." His mother leveled him with a stare before turning and sharing a look with Billy—a look that sent a shiver of apprehension down his spine.

"We've tried it your way." She gestured to Billy and rolled her eyes. No one wanted to rehash that drunken disaster.

She waved her cigarette toward Ryan, "And we've tried it your way.... the *nice* way." She didn't need to roll her eyes, the sneer was enough. "Now, it's time we do it my way."

"Ma—"

She continued as if he'd never interrupted. "We know his weakness is his wife and baby. And Daniel may be untouchable but that wife of his.... she has a past."

"I've told you, Ma, I don't think it's right to use a man's family against him."

That earned him a vicious scowl. "Daniel was no better when he took everything and left us with nothing. Do you think he cared how his actions would hurt your father's family? No. He's ruthless and he deserves the same kind of treatment."

Ryan shut his mouth. They'd had this argument before, too many times. He knew where this was going.

"She has a past. Everybody knows she was engaged to his business partner before Daniel stole her away, just like he steals everything else."

"That's old news, Ma," Billy said.

"Maybe, but no one got the whole story—how did he steal her and...." She paused to take a drag of her cigarette, which conveniently added a dramatic effect. "Who knows who's really the father of that baby?"

"Really, Ma, you're going to start gossip about an innocent baby," Ryan said. Sometimes the extent of his mother's vendetta never ceased to amaze him. There was no way he would go along it.

"Is Jack Everett the baby daddy?" Billy asked.

Their mother shrugged. "Doesn't matter. Daniel is a proud man and he loves his privacy. He'll pay to stop the talk, whether it's true or not."

And yet again, that's what it came down to. Money. That's all that mattered to his mother and brother, despite their talk of justice for their father and for their family name. It was bull, all of it. They just wanted the money they felt they were owed.

Money was all it would take. He thought of Lucia's expression when she'd pleaded with him to think of his family and how money could help them. "What if I can find another way to get us money?"

They turned to him then with gratifyingly shocked looks. "How?" his mother asked.

"It's not just about the money," Billy said.

Of course it was, but he didn't have the energy to argue. Ryan would bet everything he had that they would be satisfied once they bled some money out of Gladwell. That's what this was about for them, whether they admitted it or not. He could end this whole disastrous scheme and get back to his life. Ryan and his family could have their vengeance in the form of money—a smile started to form as he thought of Daniel's face if he learned his precious Lucia had married the bartender. Okay, sticking it to Daniel would be gratifying. And in the end, Gladwell's money would go to Ryan's family. He would get his vengeance on Daniel and his mother and brother would get their blood money.

And Lucia?

The image of those sad eyes staring up at him flashed through his mind for the millionth time. He couldn't drag her into this.

This was her idea. The devil on his shoulder had a point. She's the one who'd proposed the plan—literally. And it wasn't like she had nothing to gain. She was in it for the money. They would all get what they want.

A flicker of doubt gave him pause. If Lucia got hurt....

She wouldn't. She wouldn't even need to know his family's history or his hatred toward her relative. Much as his mother and brother might insist they need more—namely public humiliation and a smear on Daniel's good name—they would change their tune when they got their hands on his money.

And this would finally be over. His family could move on with their lives. Ivy and her baby could go about their lives without a care. And he would be free.

Well, married but free. And he was quite certain Lucia didn't intend for this to be a lifetime commitment. He could handle being married to Lucia for a couple months. How hard could it be?

His mother and brother were still staring at him, waiting for him to explain. "I need you both to trust me a little while longer. I think I have a plan."

Maybe. His own nasty words from the night before echoed in his ears. Hopefully.

Ryan shot up from the couch and grabbed his coat which was hanging over a stack of boxes as his brother's voice called out to him. "Hey, where do you think you're going?"

* * * *

Lucia's night was a disaster. Her tables were rude, the kitchen kept messing up orders, and her tips were nonexistent.

And Ryan hadn't even been there.

Not that Lucia had wanted to see him after the horrible way they'd left things, but still. She kinda had. Okay, she'd really wanted to see him, if for no other reason than to give him a piece of her mind about jumping to conclusions. Who did he think he was acting like he knew all about her and her family?

He still thought Daniel was her family. Lucia ripped off her apron. She was sick of feeling guilty about her lies of omission. She didn't owe Ryan anything. If he got that bent out of shape over Daniel, she could only imagine what he'd think once he found out she was the daughter of the wealthiest man in Italy—one of the wealthiest people in all of Europe.

But it didn't matter because he wasn't here and she wasn't going to tell him anyway. She'd learned her lesson about telling the truth.

Lucia grabbed her purse from the back room and said her goodbyes to the kitchen staff. The only other front of house employee left was the alternate bartender who hadn't been nearly as patient with Lucia's clumsiness as Ryan was. She had suffered under his judgmental glares all night, and she'd only broken one glass. *One.* Ryan would never have been so critical—he would have been nice.

That was what hurt the most about the whole situation—the fact that she'd been so wrong about him. From the moment she'd met him, he'd always seemed so sweet. There was a kindness in his eyes and a way of finding the humor no matter what was going on around him. She'd been drawn to that just as much as she'd been tempted by him physically.

For the millionth time that day, her mind flashed on the look of disdain in his eyes when he'd called her a spoiled brat. Apparently even kind, sweet Ryan couldn't see past her wealthy family. She inhaled sharply. She would *not* cry.

She wrapped her coat tightly around her as she walked out into the crisp night. The irony of her situation wasn't lost on her. The last love interest in her life was drawn to her because of her family and now this one spurned her for it. She couldn't win.

A bitterly cold wind smacked her in the face and she pulled up her hood. She hadn't gone more than two steps in the direction of her subway when she heard her name called. Whipping around she saw Ryan running toward her, his head tipped down against the wind. Her pulse started to race. *Stop it. He's probably here to yell some more. Tell you how entitled and spoiled you are.* But her mental scolding was useless. Her heart kept beating like she was running a marathon. *Dammit.*

When he reached her he stopped and they stood there for a moment, each waiting for the other to speak. "What are you doing here?" Lucia bit out

"I, uh...I wanted to see you," Ryan said, shifting from foot to foot. "I wanted to apologize."

His words coiled through her, warming her from the inside out. *He wanted to see her! He wanted to apologize!* Lucia bit her lip to keep from smiling as struggled with what to say to that. *What did that mean?*

He shoved his hands in his pockets and glanced up at her, a sheepish, apologetic little smile warming her from head to toe.

No, no, no. She would not be won over that easily. Crossing her arms over her chest, she tried her best to remain strong. "So apologize."

His smile faltered a bit at that response.

Good.

"What I said about you being a spoiled brat was rude and uncalled for." He looked at her then, as if it was her turn to talk.

Lucia stiffened. *That was it?* Apparently he picked up on her annoyed silence because he started talking again. "And the other thing...." He made a ridiculous hand gesture to her mouth and then his.

"The kiss?" she prompted.

"Yeah, that." He shoved his hands into his pockets. "That should never have happened. That was a mistake."

A mistake. All the warmth she'd felt evaporated. She was frozen to the core. Air was coming a little too quickly as her lungs struggled to keep pace with her rapidly shifting emotions as her initial excitement was replaced with a sudden and intense burst of anger and pain. So that's what he felt bad about. Kissing her. Her hands clenched at her sides as she struggled to regain control.

"You call that an apology?" she said.

Ryan straightened at the harshness in her voice.

Dammit, she hadn't meant to come across as a harpy but for the love of God, he just stood here and told her that kiss—that unbelievable, heart-melting, once-in-a-lifetime kiss had been a mistake.

And sure, maybe she had said the same thing only hours before to Holly and Ivy…but she'd lied. She'd thought it had meant something. That there was something there between them. Chemistry at the very least. For the first time in her life she'd been treated like a woman. She'd felt like a woman. And he thought it was a mistake.

"I-uh…." Ryan's eyes crinkled up in confusion. "I think maybe that came out wrong."

"No, I understand you." Lucia barely recognized the cold voice speaking. But anger was good—it was so much better than the pain that threatened to cripple her. She clung to that anger, keeping her voice even. "I get it. You feel badly that you kissed me and then called me names."

Ryan flinched. "Yeah, I mean, that's not what I intended—"

Lucia held up a hand to stop him. "I get it. But that was a terrible apology. I mean, English isn't my first language, but even I know that an apology usually involves the words '*I'm sorry*.'"

And then he did it. He tilted his head and took his hands out of his pockets so he could hold her own in his. Then he gave her that tender, sweet, kind, amazing look that made her want to curl up against him and call it home.

"Lucia," he said, his blue eyes never leaving hers. "I'm sorry."

She didn't want to cave. She could feel the anger seeping away even as she tried to grasp onto it. But there it was. The bastard stole her anger. Unfortunately all that remained was a bitter sadness, which she'd been trying to avoid and ignore for the past twenty-four hours.

"Look," she said on a sigh. "I don't need your apologies and I don't want to hear about what a mistake it was that we kissed."

He was studying her with something annoyingly close to concern but he didn't push it. Instead he reached out one hand and brushed away a lock of hair that the wind had blown across her face. "Okay then, do you want to talk about our wedding?"

Lucia froze. The wind had picked up and she was certain she'd misunderstood. Her English skills always fell short when she was emotional. Obviously he hadn't just said—

Ryan fell onto one knee with a wicked grin. "Lucia Jones. Will you make the happiest…and wealthiest…man alive and be my bride?"

Lucia's heart threatened to leap out of her chest with unexpected happiness. He was proposing. Ryan was proposing! Her hands flew to her heart as she struggled to catch her breath.

For one insane, ridiculous moment it didn't matter about money. She was just ecstatic, pure and simple. As if this was a real proposal and she was a normal girl head over heels in love.

So ridiculous. But still, her rational mind couldn't dampen her joy. If he was serious about going through with the marriage, she would have it all. Her career, her future…

And the chance to spend more time with Ryan.

That was *not* what this was about. But it was a perk, she supposed, that she had a crush on the man who was currently proposing on one knee.

She couldn't stop the laugh that escaped her. Clapping a hand over her mouth she tugged him to his feet as the clouds overhead parted and droplets of rain fell on their heads.

"Are you serious?"

Ryan nodded. "You're right. It makes sense. I mean, it's crazy but it makes sense. We both need money and a way to get it is just sitting there staring us in the face."

"Right," Lucia said. A flicker of disappointment stunned her for a moment. But that was silly—this marriage idea had always been about one thing, and one thing only. Money. Finally, she would have her dream career….and get to spend time with her crush in the meantime. Giddy excitement had her grinning up at him. "And all we have to do to get it is lie."

She tilted her head to the side, drawing a little closer so he could hear her over the rain and wind and traffic. "Somehow I don't think that should be too hard for us. What do *you* think, Ryan *Smith*?"

Chapter 7

Twenty-four hours and multiple cups of coffee later, Lucia was at a cheap, seedy motel a few blocks away from the Las Vegas Strip staring at Ryan across the divide that separated their twin beds. *Well, this was romantic.*

Ryan had his laptop sitting next to him. "So, uh, it looks like I'll need your name."

He held up the screen as if offering proof and there it was, the Clark County marriage license application. Lucia's heart took a nosedive.

This had been her idea, she reminded herself as her stomach twisted itself into a knot. She'd convinced him they had to act quickly. That time was of the essence. And it *was*. They had to get this sham of a wedding over with before her friends and family got wind of her plans and intervened. And before Ryan had a chance to change his mind. It had been her idea to jump on the next flight to Vegas. But still....

He raised a brow at her silence. "Having second thoughts?"

"No." That had come out a little too loudly if Ryan's little smile was anything to go by. Lucia flopped back against the pillows. "Okay, maybe."

It was stupid. Ridiculous, even. She was *not* a romantic. She'd never been one to sit around daydreaming about her wedding day, not even when she'd been engaged to Marco. But here, now, when she was hours away from eloping....suddenly all she could think of was what her wedding *should* be. Without even realizing she'd done it, at some point in her life she'd gone and planned it. And it wasn't in Vegas.

It had to be at the villa. Her home. And her grandfather would walk her down the aisle while her family and friends looked on. It wasn't about the dress or the decorations, it was about the people. And the person. She was supposed to marry a man she loved more than anything else in the world. He was supposed to look at her the way her grandfather looked at her grandmother when she was alive—the way Daniel looked at Ivy and the way Jack looked at Holly.

Her future husband was supposed to love her and she was supposed to love him. They were supposed to trust one another but Lucia couldn't even bring herself to tell Ryan her true last name. She didn't want to see that look of disgust on his face ever again and that's what would happen if he learned how privileged her upbringing had truly been.

Lucia blinked back tears as she stared up at the ceiling. This was not how it was supposed to be.

She heard Ryan get up and then the mattress beside her sank as he lay down beside her so they were both staring up at the ceiling. "We don't have to go through with this, you know."

Lucia continued to stare at the ceiling, which was a disgusting mural of water stains, cobwebs, and dust. Of course she didn't *have* to go through with this. No one was going to put a gun to her head and make her marry. It had been her idea. Granted, she would feel bad about the flight Ryan had just paid for but it wouldn't be the end of the world. They could return to New York, she would pay him back for the flights, and this whole thing would be forgotten.

And she would still be waiting tables while Gretchen and the others got their big breaks in the fashion world. Maybe, just maybe, she could scrimp together enough to go to school for design a year from now.

A year of waiting, drawing, sketching....for nothing and nobody. It would be her "little hobby," like Marco used to call it. Her heart twisted in pain at the thought.

She wasn't aware she'd let out a heavy sigh until Ryan mocked her by echoing with an even louder and more pitiful sigh. When she turned her head to the side to see him, she found herself looking straight into his eyes. Their faces were so close they were practically touching. His lips were right there, all she had to do was shift a little and they would meet in the middle.

But she wouldn't. This was a business arrangement, not a romantic getaway and certainly not a *real* elopement. The most efficient way to mess up this whole arrangement would be to complicate it by getting physical...again. Not that he even wanted to, he'd made it abundantly clear that he'd thought that epic kiss had been a mistake.

That line of thought brought about another sigh and this time Ryan openly laughed in her face.

"Oh, come on, princess, it's not that bad."

Princess. *Principessa.* The old nickname was as good as a slap across the face. Lucia frowned and her voice came out harsher than intended. "Don't call me that."

Ryan's brows shot up.

"Princess," she said. "Don't call me that, I hate that nickname."

Ryan turned onto his side so he was facing her. "Something tells me there's a story there."

Lucia rolled her eyes and turned her face back up toward the ceiling—the safe, not even remotely sexy, stained ceiling. "Of course there's a story there, but it's not a terribly interesting one."

"Hit me."

Lucia turned to him in surprise. "I'm sorry?"

"Hit me," he said again. And then, when she reached out and smacked his shoulder he laughed. "That's just an expression."

"Oh." She knew that. It had taken her a second though to register the meaning and in that time she realized he had given her the perfect opportunity she'd been hoping for since the moment he'd called her spoiled. Who was she to look a gift horse in the mouth?

"So," Ryan prodded. "The story?"

"It's about my family..." she started. *The family he knew nothing about.* Guilt gnawed at her.

"Even better." Ryan reached over and pushed a curl behind her ear. "We're supposed to convince people that we're madly in love and I barely know anything about you."

He had a point there. Maybe she wasn't giving him enough credit. He'd apologized for his initial response to finding out she was an heiress, perhaps it was time to be totally honest about herself and her family. They may not be a real couple but they were in a partnership of sorts. *And a partnership of any kind required trust,* she could all but hear her grandfather's voice say.

"I mean, all I know is that your name is Lucia, you hail from Italy and you're somehow related to Daniel Gladwell. Oh, and I also know that you're a terrible waitress."

"Hey!" She reached over and smacked him again for good measure. "Only two of those statements are true." She ticked them off on her finger. "My name *is* Lucia....but it's not Jones."

She laughed as Ryan pretended to be shocked by this announcement. "And the other truth?"

"I'm from Italy," she said with a roll of her eyes. "Obviously."

There was a silent pause and she glanced over to see Ryan still watching her but with an intensity that hadn't been there before. "So you're not related to Daniel Gladwell?"

Lucia laughed. "No. I don't know what he told you but he's a family friend, not my big brother, though he likes to act like it." She glanced over and added, "In his defense, he acts like an overprotective older brother with most people he cares about. Except Ivy, of course. She's the only one who keeps him in check."

Ryan was oddly silent. When she looked over his expression was unreadable. "Are you okay?"

That snapped him out of it. The friendly smile was back and it was like that momentary lapse had never happened. "Fine. Just surprised to learn you're not related to Daniel."

Her brows rose in a questioning look and he quickly added, "I mean, that's a relief. Pretty sure I wouldn't have a job in the morning if I ran away with the big boss's little sister."

Lucia couldn't help but laugh at that. They'd only talked numbers in general terms and she was fairly certain Ryan didn't really understand just how much money he would be coming into if this plan succeeded. That statement confirmed it. She'd tell him exactly how wealthy he was about to become….eventually. For now, she said, "Ryan, if we go through with this you won't need a job."

Ryan's smile only grew bigger but he didn't reply. He did however sit up and wrap one leg around her so he was effectively straddling her on the bed, his hands pinning her arms to the sides.

The suddenly intimate position left her breathless but Ryan was wearing a teasing grin and his eyes were dancing with mischief. "Tell me, my maybe, sorta, almost wife-to-be….are you ticklish?"

Lucia gasped in horror and immediately started struggling beneath him. After a few seconds of wriggling she realized that he'd gone utterly still. He was frozen above her, his hands still gripping her arms firmly. The atmosphere in the air shifted; it grew heavy and thick. Lucia sucked air into lungs that were suddenly desperate for oxygen and saw Ryan's gaze dropped to her breasts, watching the rapid rise and fall as she struggled to catch her breath. She shifted slightly beneath him before freezing. Oh God, she could feel the hard length of him pressed against her thigh.

They stayed like that, frozen like a statue, struggling for air, waiting and watching. Lucia's mind grew fuzzy with lust as her gaze focused on his lips. She waited for him to close the distance between them and just the thought of continuing that kiss was enough to leave her wet and aching.

He was so close. This was happening…it was actually happening.

And then he leapt off of her as though she'd burst into flames in his arms. Ryan was all movement, a blur of action as he paced the hotel room, grabbing a set of keys from the desk and ruffling through his duffel bag beside the bed.

"Up and at 'em, princess." His overly jovial tone was a splash of freezing cold water against her flushed and sensitive skin.

Princess. A shudder rippled through her, it was a jab in the gut on top of a slap across the face. He didn't want her. No, that wasn't true. She could still feel the hard length of him pressed against her. He did want her. He just didn't want to want her. Somehow that was even worse.

Before her addled brain could even begin to sort that one out, he was heading to the door. "I'll wait for you in the lobby," he called over his shoulder.

"Wait, where are we going?"

He was halfway through the door when he stopped and poked his head in through the open door. "You need to take your mind off of everything. Best way to make a decision is to think about something else, everybody knows that."

When she continued to stare at him, he added. "We're going out."

He slammed the door shut behind him, leaving her alone. On the bed. And horny as hell.

What. Was. That?

Lucia scrambled off the bed. So Mr. Cool wanted to act like he wasn't interested? He wanted to make her feel like she was the only one burning up over here? She opened her suitcase with far more force than necessary, sending several garments toppling over the edge. That was fine by her.

She rummaged through the clothes until she found what she was looking for and pulled it out with a triumphant grin. Two could play at this game.

* * * *

Ryan paced the lobby of their sleazy motel, trying to avoid eye contact with the night manager who was eyeing him like he was about to whip out a gun and rob the place. No robberies tonight, friend, just a man trying desperately to avoid his hot-as-hell fiancée.

He'd almost lost it back there. Almost. What had he been thinking, climbing on top of her like that when just lying beside her, not touching at all, had been a torturous exercise.

He hadn't been thinking—that was the answer. He'd been so distracted by the sadness and confusion in those beautiful eyes of her, he had stopped thinking completely. All he'd wanted to do was make her smile. Make her laugh, maybe. And instead he'd found himself hovering over her like some crazed sex fiend.

Thank God he'd stopped himself when he had. Lucia was a sweet girl. A good kid. She deserved more than a one-night stand with her fake fiancé. She deserved a real relationship, which was something he knew nothing about. And really, who could blame him, considering the role models he had growing up. His parents' relationship had been unhealthy, to say the least. Was it any wonder he'd never been able to keep a girlfriend longer than a week? The moment things got real, he got out. It was the best way to avoid the toxic atmosphere he'd been surrounded by when he was growing up.

A fiancée was not something he ever expected to have. But this was short-term. A wife for a few months? That he could handle. He would just have to develop some self-control. One thing was for sure, he would be taking a lot of cold showers before this marriage was over.

He could do this. He could keep his hands to himself and keep her out of his family's drama. She may come from money and she obviously had some connection to Daniel but she wasn't Daniel and there was no way he was going to make her pay for his mistakes.

How are you going to keep her out of it? She's already in it.

He could practically hear his brother's snide, cynical voice in his ear, mocking him for his naiveté. And maybe his brother's voice was right. Maybe he'd gone too far to pull back now. Maybe he would drag Lucia into this mess after all...

No. He could keep her out of this. If he just kept to his plan, he would have it all.

And what was his plan? Well...he was still working on it. But one thing was clear, if he could get Lucia to go through with this sham of a wedding, he could get his family back the money they'd lost. Or at least enough that his mother and brother could get a fresh start. Ryan wouldn't keep any of it—he'd already decided that. His payment would come from being free from them. He could make his own way in the world once they let him go.

Maybe the money would be enough for them. He could just imagine Billy's mocking laughter.

If it wasn't enough, he would use his connection to Lucia to blackmail Daniel into an apology, at the very least. Watching the high and mighty Daniel admit that he'd been in the wrong when he stole their father's company out from under him was all he'd ever wanted from the man, personally. He'd never liked the idea of taking Daniel's blood money, he just wanted to hear him apologize.

An apology plus the money *should* be enough to appease his family. Doubts still niggled at his conscience but he shoved them aside.

The tightness in his chest began to dissipate as he paced the lobby. He could do this. He could end a decade's worth of hate and anger….and he could protect Lucia from any real harm while he did it.

His inner pep talk was interrupted by the sound of the elevator doors opening. Ryan turned and then stopped. The air rushed from his lungs as his blood raced to his groin.

Oh, holy hell.

Lucia was a vision—a Victoria's Secret model straight off the runway. Clad in an itty-bitty black gauzy sheath dress that stopped high up her thigh, exposing her lean, tan legs, which ended in heels that looked impossibly high and insanely sexy. The dress brushed against her curves as she walked toward him, not so tight as to reveal everything but revealing enough that his mouth was watering with her every move.

When she drew close she stopped and paused in a model pose. "What do you think?"

"Uhhhh." Was that a word that came out of his mouth? He didn't think so. It sounded more like a groan and Lucia's answering smile was mocking.

She'd gone all out with the makeup. Gone was the fresh-faced girl next door. She'd done something to her eyes to make them look smoky and her lips were a vibrant, siren red. Her dark wavy hair was loose around her shoulders in a tousled, morning-after kind of way that had his brain flashing on all sorts of ways he could woo her back to their hotel room.

He swallowed thickly and tried again. "You look amazing."

Lucia took a step closer and wrapped her hand around his arm. "Thank you. Shall we?"

He let her lead him out into the crisp desert night air, which did nothing to clear his lust-filled brain or ease the tension in his body. If anything, the night air brought with it whiffs of her tantalizingly delicate, floral perfume and every once in a while her arm would brush against his and every nerve ending would stand on edge, waiting for another touch.

All the while, she led him closer to the noise and action of The Strip. She strode purposefully in those damned high heels….as though she knew exactly where they were going.

"Where are you taking us?" he asked.

She gave him a sideways glance and a coy smile. "Out." When he continued to stare at her, she added, "You're the one who said I needed a distraction."

He eyed her openly now. "So we're….what? Going dancing?"

She gave a little huff of a laugh. "We're in Vegas, baby," she drawled in a ridiculously cute and over-the-top American accent. "We're going gambling."

He paused and then had to hurry to keep pace wither her. How a petite woman with sky-high stilettos could move so quickly was a mystery for another day.

"With what money?" A knot of tension had formed in his gut at the word "gambling."

She ignored him, apparently too busy gazing up at the billboards and fluorescent signs that were starting to come into view now that they were getting close to the action.

"With what?" he asked again, the anxiety making his tone harsher than he'd intended. "You and I spent every last penny we had getting out here."

She tossed her hair and laughed—she *laughed.* "I've got some ones in my wallet. That should be enough to get us started."

Two hours later, Ryan stared in awe as Lucia raked in another batch of quarters into her giant plastic cup.

"How did you do that?"

Lucia ignored him as she sifted through the change, her brows furrowed in concentration as she tried to add up her winnings. "Do what?" she asked absently.

She'd barely paid any attention to him since they'd arrived. From the moment they'd walked in the door she'd been in the zone—weirdly all business while still laughing and chatting with the gamblers around her at the penny slots, and then the nickel slots and now the quarter slots.

She'd been on fire from the very start. And he….well, he'd been a ball of nerves. He normally prided himself on being cool and laid back but God almighty, he hated everything about the casinos—from the stench of cigarettes to the noisy dings and bells of the slot machines. But more than anything, he hated the nauseous sensation he got every time she went back for more.

She looked up at him then with a satisfied smile. Holding up her bucket of winnings, she said, "That should do it."

Relief rushed through him. That was it. They were done. They could go home…or back to their seedy motel. At this point, he'd take it. "Perfect," he said, a little louder than intended. "Let's go cash that in and go grab some dinner with those winnings of yours."

Lucia stood too but she was shaking her head. "We can't leave yet, I'm just getting started."

"What do you mean, you're just getting—"

But she was already halfway to the exit.

* * * *

His lucky charm—that was what her grandfather used to call her. She couldn't help it and she sure as hell couldn't explain it. Maybe it was a self-fulfilling prophecy or maybe it was fate. All she knew was—she'd always been lucky.

She could hear Ryan behind her, jostling his way through the crowd to keep up with her but she didn't slow down. Racking up some change at the slots had been nice and all but Lucia had a wedding to pay for. Which meant....

"Where are we going?" Ryan had reached her side and was scowling at her, something he'd been doing quite a lot of since they'd stepped foot in their first casino.

"I am going to the poker tables." She watched his face fall. "But you don't have to come with me."

Ryan's jaw set but he still kept pace beside her as they moved past a group of drunken bachelorette partygoers. One girl was wearing a telltale tiara and Lucia couldn't help but stare at the bride-to-be. Sadness washed over her again like a wave and she inhaled deeply. Now was not the time to get sappy about childhood dreams. There would be plenty of time for fairytale weddings and falling in love once her career was built and she and Ryan got their divorce.

But still, a nagging voice was making it hard to concentrate on anything other than her grandfather's disappointment once he found out. For a world-class romantic who believed in fairytale endings, an elopement for money was hardly something to be proud of. What would her mother have thought? Would she have applauded the fact that she was finally doing something on her own, far away from grandfather's smothering and Marco's lecturing? Was she rooting her on from beyond the grave, hoping her daughter would be a success where she had failed? Or would she be horrified that her daughter was falling for a gold digger, just like she had done? That thought made her stomach turn.

But this was different. Ryan was nothing like her father. He may be a gold digger but in a sense so was she. And at least he was open and honest about it. She may have been untrusting and secretive, but her soon-to-be husband wasn't.

Ryan tugged her arm, pulling her out of the walkway and into an alcove filled with slot machines and gamblers who looked hypnotized by the bright lights. "You don't have to do this," Ryan said. "You've already made more than enough. Why test your luck?"

Lucia held up the cup and gave it a little shake. "This is luck." She pointed toward the card tables. "That is talent."

Ryan rolled his eyes.

"Okay, fine, there's some luck involved. But I know what I'm doing, I swear. I grew up playing poker with my grandfather and uncles."

His brows rose. She shrugged. It wasn't a typical childhood pastime, but then, little about her childhood had been normal. She'd been too young to fit in with her aunts and uncles and too old for the rest of her cousins so she'd always alternated between being treated like one of the adults or as the go-to babysitter.

Ryan looked miserable. She reached out a hand and laid it on his arm. "You don't have to stay. I'll be fine."

One side of his lips turned up in a wry smile. "And leave you here… alone…looking like this?"

Heat flushed her cheeks at the openly admiring gaze he swept over her. His initial reaction had been extremely satisfying but hearing him admit she was tempting gave her a heady, dizzy feeling.

Meeting his eyes in that smoke-filled, noisy room, it dawned on her. She had a crush on her fiancé. A little giggle escaped her at the thought and Ryan gave her a questioning look.

She shook her head. It was nothing. It would pass. They would get married, as planned, wait as long as it took to sort out the trust fund and divvy up the money and then they would get divorced.

But who was to say she couldn't have fun in the meantime?

She took a step closer. "You think I'm that irresistible, huh?"

His Adam's apple bobbed up and down as he swallowed. She took a step closer so they were touching, her legs brushing against his, and she lightly wrapped her arms around his neck.

"Lucia." Her name sounded like a warning and a thrill shot through her. She'd never been a temptress before. She liked it.

But he looked miserable. He had from the moment they'd stepped foot in the first casino. Despite the fact that she was having a blast, she couldn't in all good conscience, keep torturing this man.

Her fiancé.

She sucked in air as excitement and terror washed over her. Was she really doing this?

Ryan's eyes were studying her and for one blissful moment she got swept away in the endless kindness she saw there.

"Are you okay?" His voice was low but despite the noise around them, she could hear him as though he'd whispered in her ear. His arms wrapped around her, safe and strong. To the outside world they must look like a couple. Like a real, legitimate couple taking a moment to cuddle during a night out on the town.

What if this was real?

The fantasy was tempting. There was concern and tenderness in his gaze. He cared about her. It would be all too easy to let herself forget reality— to imagine that he was her boyfriend. For real.

A sigh escaped her. But he wasn't. Not yet at least. At the moment he was just her co-worker and maybe-friend and he was with her for her money.

What else was new?

No, she couldn't judge Ryan. Not when she'd talked him into it and not when she was using him for the very same reason. She had a chip on her shoulder and it was time she got over it.

Starting now, with this man. He was trusting her to hold up her end of this bargain and she would trust him as well.

With that thought, she unwrapped her arms and took a step back. Tilting her chin up so she could look him in the eyes, she said, "You're miserable here, Ryan. Why don't you go back to the hotel and finish our application and take it to the Clark County Marriage Bureau."

"This late?"

She lifted his wrist to check out the time. "It's open till midnight. You have plenty of time."

A small smile gave her a glimpse of those amazing dimples. "We're really doing this, huh?"

Lucia nodded, the butterflies in her stomach making it difficult to speak. Was he as terrified as she was? "We're really doing this."

She turned to head to the poker tables but he stopped her. "Will you be okay here alone?"

Rolling her eyes, she put one hand on her hip and cocked her head to the side. "When am I not okay?"

He laughed but stopped her one more time. "Aren't you forgetting something? I still need to know your name if I'm going to complete that application."

Maggie Dallen

Lucia froze, her temporary sense of confidence wavering for a bit. This was it. Her secret would be out there.

Trust, she reminded herself. *This was it.* "Brunelli. I'm Lucia Brunelli."

Chapter 8

Brunelli. Where had he heard that name before?

It had been nagging at him as he walked back to the motel and the entire time he'd completed the form and now, as he waited in line for the county clerk's office to file the license, he gave in to temptation and searched the name on his smartphone.

Whoa. Article after article came up and he scrolled through them, skimming the opening sentences and catch phrases. "One of the wealthiest families in Europe," "manufacturing tycoon," "Italian royalty." He sucked in air as the reality of her background became clear. She hadn't been exaggerating when she'd described herself as an heiress. If anything, she'd been being humble. The Brunellis were a living, breathing dynasty.

He couldn't help himself. Curiosity got the best of him so next he searched "Daniel Gladwell" and "Brunelli" and there it was. They were business partners. They'd come together to form EverTech. Even Ryan knew about that company and he knew nothing about the tech world. Only someone living under a rock didn't know about Jack Everett's new company but Ryan hadn't realized that it had been backed by Gladwell. And, apparently, Lucia's family. He took a closer look at the picture of Gianni Brunelli. Too old to be her father. Grandfather maybe?

His fingers hovered over the keyboard on his phone. He was tempted to type in Lucia's full name to see what came up but something stopped him. Somehow that seemed like an invasion of privacy.

High morals coming from someone who's using her as an in to get revenge on her family friend.

He wasn't going to go through this again. He'd made his decision. Besides, he would keep her from getting hurt. There was no way he'd let his family drag Lucia into this. He would give them the money and he would force an apology out of Daniel—let him know that he and his family finally had the upper hand. And that would be it.

He and Lucia would go their separate ways once the money was handed over and his battle would be over. He would be free. And Lucia? Well, she would have her dream business, her very own fashion line.

Win-win.

The harried clerk behind the counter called out his name. He was up.

* * * *

Hours had passed and Ryan found it hard to believe that Lucia could still be where he'd left her but there she was, looking far too gorgeous as she leaned back in her seat and studied her hand.

God, she was beautiful. And she was about to become his wife.

He nearly burst out in hysterical laughter for the millionth time that day. *What the hell was he doing?*

He studied her as she studied her cards. Her expression gave nothing away but the stack of chips in front of her was a clear sign that she'd been having a successful night. Was there anything this woman couldn't do?

Well, waitressing. But other than that.

The woman sitting at that card table was a force of nature. From the moment she'd entered his life, she'd been a source of energy and passion. A vivid, sparkling ball of energy in his otherwise gray and bleak world.

And he got to marry her and share in her ridiculous wealth.

Of all the bars in all the cities.... Ryan was sure as hell glad she'd walked into his.

She won the hand and Ryan was pretty sure the sun came out in the casino as her smile of elation lit up the room. She spotted him then as she leaned over to collect her winnings and his heart threatened to burst out of his rib cage as the full force of her smile hit him in the gut.

He was in over his head.

Shaking off that thought, he moved to her side and glared at two men who were openly ogling her ass as she leaned over.

He helped her gather up the chips and as soon as they walked away from the table and out of earshot, he said, "Jesus, Lucia. How much money did you win?"

She laughed at that and it sounded absurdly bright and innocent considering they were in a casino in Vegas in the middle of the night.

"That's just from the last hour," she said.

He turned to face her. "Did you cash out the rest already?"

Her lips puckered up in an impish grin. "You could say that."

With that cryptic statement, she led the way toward the main hallway that connected the casino to the hotel.

"Where are we going?"

A hotel employee was waiting at a doorway and his face lit up when he caught sight of Lucia. She waved to the young man, who looked smitten.

"Friend of yours?" he muttered.

"Alfie has been kind enough to help me with the planning," she said. "Isn't that right, Alfie?"

Alfie bore a striking resemblance to an overeager puppy as he all but panted with joy at Lucia's praise. "I try, Lucy."

Lucy?

"Planning....what?" he asked.

At that, Alfie opened the door he'd been blocking. Ryan and Lucia walked into the room....and into their wedding.

"You have got to be kidding me." The words slipped out under his breath as he took in the garish room which was covered in flowers and streamers and more glitter than he'd ever thought possible. But the kicker of it all....the feature that made him certain he was dreaming....was Elvis.

"You hired an Elvis impersonator?" It was a stupid question. A rhetorical question. Because there, right in front of him, was the King himself, in all his opulent, rhinestoned glory.

Lucia was beaming up at him. "He's great, right?"

"Great," he repeated, more out of shock than in agreement. "And the, uh..." He gestured around him at the sparkling chaos. "This was all you?"

"Oh no," Lucia said with a laugh. "The disco ball and shag carpeting were already here. Alfie helped with the flowers and streamers. What do you think?"

She looked so happy, all he could say was, "It's perfect."

And it was. The nervous panicky feeling in his gut dissolved in the face of this ridiculousness. How could anyone take this wedding seriously when a middle-aged man dressed up in sequins was performing the ceremony? She had done it. She'd managed to make their wedding....perfect.

Her head fell back as she laughed. "I knew you'd love it. I figured, if we're going to elope in Vegas, we might as well embrace it, right?"

She looked so unbelievably beautiful standing in that gaudy room, her eyes bright with laughter and—

He was marrying this woman.

Even if it was just a fraud, for one moment he was the luckiest man alive. "It's perfect. All of it."

She shrugged as she took his arm. "I have to admit, I was a little sad to not have my fairytale wedding. But this...this is almost as good."

"You'll still have your fairytale wedding," he felt compelled to say. "Someday."

With another man. Someone who loved her and who she loved in return. For one moment, Ryan experienced a jolt of blinding, insane jealousy toward this faceless stranger. The one who would marry her for real.

Holy crap. Ryan almost tripped over his own feet as a horrible realization hit him. He was falling for Lucia.

She shrugged as she led him slowly but surely down the aisle. "Maybe someday I'll get the fairytale. But first, I get to marry you. In front of God, Alfie, the organist, and Elvis."

"Organist?" He glanced over his shoulder to see an old woman with purple hair waving from the corner before she launched into a rousing rendition of "Here Comes the Bride."

* * * *

Lucia's wedding went by in a blur. Her heart pounded in her ears as Elvis talked and talked for what felt like an eternity.

Lucia kept her eyes on Ryan as Elvis said the magic words. "I now pronounce you man and wife."

Alfie started clapping from his front row seat and the organist played "Viva Las Vegas" with gusto. And Ryan and Lucia continued to stare at one another.

What had they done?

"You may now kiss the bride," Elvis added.

Ryan hesitated and Lucia found herself holding her breath. But then he smiled at her and her knees went weak. She would never tire of that smile. He leaned over and she was pretty sure she heard him say, "What the hell" before his lips met hers and for the first time in what felt like forever the nerves that had been making her feel like she was in a shaky cage all day ceased to rattle and a calm swept over her as her mind went blissfully blank.

It was a light, sweet, gentle kiss—nothing like the passionate makeout session they'd had before. And it was perfect. Tears came to her eyes at the tenderness of it. He pulled back and she resisted the urge to cling to him. "What now, wife?"

What now? Her plan hadn't gone beyond this point. The future suddenly seemed like a giant black hole. She was married. Now what?

"Um...."

He took her hand. "Drinks. We definitely need drinks."

They said their goodbyes to the wedding party before racing back toward the hotel lobby, which housed a rodeo-themed bar. The maître d' handed them cowboy hats as they entered and Ryan winked at her. Now they were dressing up like cowboys after being married by Elvis?

Sure, why not?

One drink turned to two, and then three. And then Lucia lost track.

"To my bride!" Ryan raised his glass and the entire bar erupted into cheers and applause. Word of their wedding had spread quickly and every time she set down her glass it seemed somebody new was offering to buy them a round.

Ryan turned to tap his glass against hers which, she discovered, was almost empty again. "We did it, Princess."

His dimpled grin was so adorable that she almost forgave him the use of her least favorite nickname. "I told you not to call me that."

His brow furrowed in drunken confusion for a minute before understanding dawned. "Oh yeah. Sorry. So what's the deal with that? Why do you hate it?"

Her mouth clamped shut automatically but he leaned in so he was in her space, his elbows resting on the bar inches away from her own. "Is that what your ex called you?"

She tried to imagine Marco calling her anything cutesy like that and had to laugh. "No. He's never called me anything but Lucy my whole life."

Ryan raised one eyebrow at that. "What was he, your high school sweetheart or something?"

"More like my junior high sweetheart. We were joined at the hip from then on. Up until a few months ago when I called off our engagement."

"That's a long time to be with someone." He was watching her carefully, like she might burst into tears at any moment. He, like everyone else, seemed to think she was heartbroken over the breakup. How could she explain that she wasn't? And neither was Marco, she'd bet her life on it. His pride was hurt and for a man like Marco, that was even worse. Heartbreak he could stand, but a blow to his ego? Something told her they wouldn't be chatting as friends anytime soon. That thought was painful in its own right. They may not have had a passionate romance but they had always loved each other dearly...as friends. She just wished she'd realized earlier that what she'd thought was a relationship was really just well laid plans and everyone else's expectations.

"He's better off without me." His eyes widened with surprise and she realized how that sounded. "Not that I was mean to him or anything. But he deserves to be with someone who really loves him. He should marry his soul mate."

Ryan took another swig of his drink. "That's awfully romantic talk for someone who just married for money."

Lucia let out a derisive snort. "I'm definitely not the romantic in my family. You should meet my grandfather."

"The billionaire tycoon, I take it?"

She paused with her drink halfway to her lips and swallowed down the sense of panic. He didn't look angry or disgusted. "You've been doing your homework."

He held his hands up in mock surrender. "Guilty. But in my defense, I think I had a right to know who I was marrying."

"Fair enough. And what about you, Ryan *Brentworth*?" She narrowed her eyes at him with feigned suspicion. "If that's really your name."

She saw his eyes widen in surprise at the mention of his name. "What?" she asked, all innocence. "I took a peek at the marriage certificate. I too wanted to know who I was marrying."

Was that a flinch? He shifted in his seat and she dropped the teasing tone. "It's kind of obvious why I used a fake name but what's your story?"

He paused for a second before his shook his head. "I told you, my family has issues. I like to keep my distance."

That wasn't all there was to it. The hesitation was brief but she caught it. Jabbing a finger at his chest, she said, "Okay, spill. What's your dirty little secret?"

Rather than answer, he took a sip of his drink. Lucia leaned back in her barstool with a groan. "Oh, come on. You know my secret."

His gaze found hers over the rim of his glass. "So…what? You're telling me that being the granddaughter of the wealthiest man in Italy is your deep, dark secret?"

She paused at that. "Yeah, I guess it is." Her eyes widened in excitement. "Although now I can add 'secretly eloped with a man I barely knew' to my list."

His smile was contagious and for a moment she allowed herself to enjoy his company. Thanks to the drinks she'd finally stopped obsessing about what was going to happen next.

The wedding night. What did he expect? Did he even want her? More importantly, what did *she* want?

Who was she kidding, she knew what she wanted and he was sitting right next to her. Was it smart to hook up with her husband? Probably not. Would she do it anyway? *Hell yes.*

Nervous excitement left her breathless. She was really going to do this. She was going to make love to her husband.

He motioned to her now-empty glass. "You need another?"

She shook her head. "I don't think I need anymore." Locking her gaze with his she added, "I think I'm ready to go back to the room."

The air grew hot and heavy between them as she waited for him to respond. She thought he might make a joke, or talk about needing to get some sleep but instead…he closed the gap between them and kissed her.

The bar faded away and not even the mechanical bull or its cheering crowd could intrude on their blissful little world. A sigh escaped her as his lips lightly moved over hers and his tongue flicked out to lightly lick her bottom lip.

She moved closer and intensified the kiss, not caring where she was or who was watching. All that mattered was getting closer to this man. He responded to her urgency by sliding his hand beneath her hair so he was cupping the back of her head, holding her to him as the kiss intensified and deepened.

The sound of one of their bar neighbors shouting out "get a room" finally forced them to part. Ryan's eyes were dark with desire and he let out of low groan when she slipped a hand onto his thigh. "Should we?" she asked.

His dazed look was gratifying as was his apparent inability to string words together. "Should we…" he echoed. "What?"

"Get a room." She couldn't believe her own nerve and she was breathless with anticipation and excitement. She'd never done anything like this before but something about this man made her feel like she could do anything…be anybody. And right now, at this particular moment … she wanted to be *bad*.

He leaned forward until his forehead was touching hers. "Hell yes."

She would have laughed if she wasn't so turned on she thought she might melt into the floor. "Okay then. Let's get out of here."

He grabbed her by the hand and led the way toward the door of the bar. He started heading toward the exit but she had a better idea. Pulling him along behind her she all but ran to the front desk. "How much for a room tonight?"

"What are you doing?" Ryan whispered in her ear.

She flashed him a smile over her shoulder. "I think we deserve something a little better than that seedy motel for our honeymoon, don't you?"

Ryan laughed and leaned in so only she could hear. "Good idea. I don't think I could make it that far without kissing you again. And when I do…."

Lucia's breath caught in her throat and when the clerk at the front desk went to get them their room keys, Lucia turned and planted a kiss on his lips. "You were saying?"

She spun back around in time to give the clerk a friendly smile when she returned but Ryan grabbed her hips and pulled her back so she was pressed against him. "You're going to pay for that."

"Promises, promises," she sang under her breath.

As soon as the clerk took their money and handed over the key cards they were laughing and kissing their way to the elevators.

There was a hum in the air that had nothing to do with the noises of the slot machines in the casino and everything to do with the feel of Ryan's hands on her hips, on her back, running up and down her arm as he raced her to the elevators.

Ryan punched the elevator button and then spun around to face her and pulled her up against him. She pressed herself even closer, loving the feel of his hard chest beneath her hands and his hands on the small of her back.

"Are you ready for your wedding night?" Ryan asked.

She opened her mouth to speak but before she could she was interrupted by a familiar voice calling out her name.

Oh no. This could not be happening.

"Lucia!" It was Holly. Lucia didn't even have to turn around; she would recognize her friend's voice anywhere. And if Holly was here, that meant Jack...

"Lucy," Jack called out in an over-the-top Ricky Ricardo voice. "You've got a lot of explaining to do."

Chapter 9

Ryan nearly toppled over as Lucia pushed him away from her as she spun around to face her friends. Ryan spotted a blonde heading toward them with a huge grin, her curls bouncing around her head. Behind her was…well, it was a face anyone would recognize since it seemed to be everywhere these days. Jack Everett—media sensation and, supposedly some sort of tech genius.

They were both walking straight toward them but Jack looked far less friendly than the blonde, who had just reached Lucia and swept her up in a tight hug. "Oh, so good to see you!" she squealed. She pulled back to face Lucia. "I take it congratulations are in order?"

Jack reached the blonde's side and wrapped an arm around her shoulders while continuing to glare at Lucia. "Lucia Antoinette Brunelli, what do you think—"

Lucia cut him off. "That's not my middle name."

Jack waved her off. "Doesn't matter."

"I think what Jack's trying to say is your grandfather…" Holly started.

Lucia finished for her. "Grandpa is worried about me."

Awkward silence reigned for a moment as Jack and Holly shared a look that confirmed what she'd said. Ryan hated the pain that suddenly filled Lucia's expression. "I didn't mean to hurt him, I just—" She stopped and sighed. "I didn't want him to find out like this."

"How *did* he find out?" Ryan asked. All three turned to him in surprise and Ryan realized that until that moment he had been largely forgotten.… even by his bride.

Now he was the center of attention and Ryan was acutely aware of Jack's assessing glare. But that was nothing compared to the unnerving way Holly was staring him down.

"Yeah, how did Grandpa find out? And how did you two find us?" Lucia asked. Some of the tension in Ryan's chest eased when he noticed that her expression had gone from pained to suspicious. He hated to see her hurting.

Jack wrapped an arm around Lucia's shoulders in a brotherly hug. "I will tell you everything, my sweet little runaway, just as soon as Holly and I get a room."

And so, about twenty minutes later, Ryan found himself and his new wife in Jack and Holly's suite on their wedding night.

He glanced over at Lucia who was perched on the edge of an overstuffed chair, looking adorably tired as she stifled a yawn. He could relate. Now that the adrenaline rush had passed and the desire had been given a cold shower, so to speak, he was ready to call this crazy day over.

Jack was fixing a drink for himself and Holly, who was still watching him in that disconcerting way. They still hadn't answered Lucia's questions and instead seemed hell bent on changing the topic, chattering on about everything from Holly's niece to their upcoming trip to Asia.

At one point, just as Ryan thought he might lose the battle with sleep and pass out then and there on these strangers' couch, Holly turned to him. "I left a suitcase in the car downstairs. Do you think you could help me bring it up?"

He noticed Lucia eyeing her friend with suspicion but Ryan agreed. How could he not?

Once in the elevator alone with Holly, she turned to him and all the sweetness and light was gone. Before him stood an avenging angel.

Oh no.

"So, Ryan *Brentworth*," she said, drawing out his last name pointedly. "Want to tell me what the hell you're doing with my friend?"

* * * *

"Okay, what was that about?" Lucia asked as she watched Holly usher Ryan out of the room.

Jack plopped down into the loveseat across from her with a weary sigh that echoed how she felt. The alcohol was wearing off and the day was catching up to her.

"What's going on, Jack?"

He met her gaze and his was filled with understanding. "I was going to ask you the same question, Luce."

Leaning back, she let her gritty eyes close for a moment before launching into the story. She left nothing out. At this point, it felt good to have a friend to confide in. When she was done, she opened her eyes to see Jack studying her. "If you needed money so badly, why didn't you come to me?"

The hurt in his voice was a kick in the gut.

"It's nothing personal, I just….this is something I wanted to do for myself. I knew you would give me money if I needed it, and so would Danny—"

"And so would your grandfather," Jack pointed out.

Lucia nodded. It was true. Her grandfather would have relented and given her anything she'd asked for, even if he thought her dream was ridiculous. But that wasn't the point. How to explain what it meant to her to do it on her own?

"My whole life, my grandfather has given me everything. He took me in when my mother couldn't raise me on her own. He raised me almost single-handedly after my mother and grandmother passed away when I was a baby…."

"But?" Jack said.

"But I'm a grown up now and he doesn't see that. He still sees me as a little girl who can't do anything for herself."

Jack looked like he was going to interrupt and she hurried on. "I know he means well but I need to do something on my own. Granted, I haven't earned the trust fund money, but it's still mine. And I need to stand on my own two feet or I'm going to end up…" She didn't finish. She couldn't.

"Like your mother." Jack was looking at her with something dangerously close to pity.

Her head jerked with a little nod. She hated admitting that even to herself, let alone anyone else but it was the truth. She was terrified of making the same mistakes her mother made. Her grandparents and the rest of her extended family had gone to great lengths to protect her from the full story of her mother's tragic story, but she'd been able to piece most of it together on her own.

Her mother had tried to stand on her own two feet. Like Lucia, she'd wanted to see the world beyond their Italian village, she'd wanted freedom and adventure. She was the "wild child" according to her aunts and uncles. So she'd gone off on her own…but she couldn't make it. She'd made one mistake after another and finally, when she couldn't take it anymore, she gave up on having a life of her own and came crawling back to Italy with an illegitimate daughter and nothing else. She'd died a year later of cancer, heartbroken and miserable…and a complete and utter failure.

That would *not* be her story.

Leaning forward, she tried to explain to Jack. "I know what I'm doing. I'm good at what I do. I know I can be a success if I can just have my shot. But I have to do it on my own."

Jack nodded but he wiped a hand over his face and Lucia saw the dark circles under his eyes. "I get that, Lucia, I do. It's not you I don't trust."

There was a heavy silence in the room as she studied Jack's unusually serious expression.

"How much do you know about this guy?"

She answered with a question of her own. "How did you know I was here?"

Jack flopped back with a groan. "You look like I feel. What do you say we hold off on the interrogations until tomorrow and get some sleep?"

Her eyes felt like sandpaper and as much as she wanted answers, she was rapidly losing the battle with sleep. "I have to find Ryan." Her husband. Who was currently off with Holly who had been acting odd as well.

Somebody needed to give her some answers. That was her last thought before sleep claimed her.

* * * *

Worst. Wedding night. Ever.

Ryan sat across the booth from Holly and watched her dive in to a pile of pancakes at the breakfast-all-day diner she'd found in the casino next to theirs. She'd insisted on eating before they could talk and so Ryan found himself sitting across from a woman who was not his wife when he should have been alone in a hotel room with Lucia.

To say that he was not a happy camper was the understatement of the century. Add to that the looming hangover, sheer exhaustion and the fact that this lunatic across from him had refused to tell him what she knew until she'd eaten a mountain of carbohydrates....

"That's it." A few patrons looked their way and Ryan lowered his voice. "We got you your pancakes so tell me what you're doing here."

Holly took another bite and continued to stare. If she was trying to psyche him out, she was succeeding. She hadn't said anything more about his last name or how they'd tracked him down but she'd been eyeing him like he was some sort of criminal mastermind since they'd met.

"Daniel called us," she finally said. "You know Daniel, don't you? He is your boss, after all." There was a tense silence before she added, "And the man who bought your family's company when it went under."

Ryan stiffened. There it was. A million responses seemed to rip through him at once. The urge to explain himself battled with anger at her presumptuous tone. As if she had any clue.

Family pride won out, like it always did. "The company didn't go under, it was a hostile takeover." He struggled to keep calm despite his brother and mother's voices screaming in his ear. Daniel Gladwell had ruined everything. That had been his family's motto since he was a kid. "My family would have recovered and kept the company running if it wasn't for Daniel."

Holly seemed nonplussed by his anger. "Uh huh."

Of course she didn't understand. He was her brother-in-law, after all, a fact he'd pieced together on the way over here. Somehow over the past few years Daniel had become a sort of saint in the press. They covered his wedding and his daughter's birth and the launching of EverTech... but no one talked about the people he put out of business when he swept in to companies that were down on their luck. No one ever talked about the failures who were left with nothing after Daniel stole it all from them.

"I'm going to ask you again," Holly said. "What are you doing with my friend?"

"Aside from marrying her?" He was oddly pleased that his joking comment made her slam down her coffee mug. Good. He was tired of being the only one pissed off around here.

She leaned over so far that her T-shirt came dangerously close to taking a dip in the whipped cream atop her pancakes. Jabbing her fork in his direction, she said, "You clearly have a grudge against Daniel and I really don't care why. That's not my business. Daniel can handle himself. But Lucia...I swear to God, if you hurt that girl—"

"I'm not going to hurt her." His entire body tensed with conviction. She must have seen that he was being honest or maybe she'd caught the fear in his voice. Not that he was afraid of her—it was difficult to be afraid of anyone who was eating pancakes, no matter how fiercely they were stabbing the air with utensils. But the idea of hurting Lucia, whether intentional or not....well, this woman had hit a nerve. He was overly defensive and he knew it. *Keep it together, Ryan.*

He tried again. "I'm not going to hurt her."

"Lucia has nothing to do with Daniel's business deals—"

"I know that." His interruption went unnoticed.

"She's a sweet kid—"

"She is *not* a kid."

"And she deserves better than this," Holly continued.

"Better than what?"

That question seemed to stump her and he took advantage of her momentary silence. "I agreed to go along with this marriage plan because it's what Lucia wanted. This was *her* idea."

Holly's eyes widened but then she scoffed. "So, what? You're not getting anything out of this deal? You're just going along with this crazy scheme out of the goodness of your heart?"

"Of course not." Now it was Ryan's turn to scoff. "I'm getting money out of this 'crazy scheme.' Lots of it."

"Oh." Holly didn't sound convinced and she stabbed at another bite with far more force than necessary. She glared at him while she chewed and Ryan resisted the urge to walk away.

One thing was clear. This woman knew enough about his past to cause him trouble. She could go to Lucia with this and he would never have a chance to explain. She would twist everything and Lucia would think....

Oh no. Lucia was alone. With Jack. If Holly knew his secrets than Jack almost certainly did as well. "Is Jack telling Lucia about me?"

God, he hated how that sounded. Like he was in grade school and afraid of being ratted out to the principal.

Holly looked too smug for her own good and she didn't answer. Instead she continued her interrogation. "Are you going to sit there and tell me that it's all a coincidence? That you just happen to be lying about your last name and working for a man you clearly despise...."

"Of course not." He spit the words out in annoyance. "But Lucia has nothing to do with my issues with Daniel. I won't let her be dragged into it."

She eyed the gaudy plastic ring he wore with impossibly wide eyes. "Are you kidding me? Something tells me *your wife* is already in this, whether she knows it or not."

Guilt gnawed at him.

Like an animal that senses blood, she went in for the kill. "Are you telling me you have no intention of using Lucia's relationship with Daniel against her?"

Dammit. "Not against *her*..." he started. And even he could hear how weak that argument was. He tried again. "Look, I like Lucia." Not *that* was the understatement of the century. "I care about her," he continued. *Better.*

Holly raised a cynical brow but she didn't interrupt.

Ryan raked a hand through his hair. How to explain? To Holly, but also...how would he explain to Lucia? The fact that he'd thought he could get through this without her learning the truth about him and his family....what a fool.

He let out a loud sigh. "Has Jack told Lucia about me?"

Holly's expression went from fierce to something disturbingly close to pity. "Not yet. We wanted to see what the situation was first and give you a chance to explain. This right here? This is your chance so try not to blow it."

His eyes narrowed as he studied her. They never had answered his earlier questions. "How did you know we were here? Lucia didn't tell anyone what we were doing."

"Daniel." Holly toyed with the whipped cream that was rapidly melting.

Of course it was Daniel. He swallowed back the bitterness. "He knows who I am?"

Holly nodded. "He took an interest in you when you tried to stand up for Lucia when you thought she was going to be deported." Suddenly she was beaming at him over her steaming mug of coffee. "That was really sweet, by the way." She waved her fork like a fairy godmother would wave a wand. "That's why we decided we should hear your side of the story first. See, we know you're not *all* bad."

"Gee, thanks."

She ignored his sarcasm. "Once Daniel realized you were using a fake name, he got suspicious so he had you followed. When he found out you two were headed to Vegas together, well....just be glad he called me and Jack and not the National Guard."

Holly's phone vibrated on the table between them. She glanced at it and then back up at Ryan. "Seems your wife is passed out cold in our hotel room."

Ryan's heart actually ached. He wanted to be with her more than anything in the world. If she was sleeping, he wanted to be by her side. He wanted to hold her and tell her that they hadn't made a mistake and that it would all be okay. He actually wanted to come clean about everything so he could make it right.

What the hell was wrong with him? Their marriage was in name only. Putting a ring on her finger didn't magically make love appear.

Maybe it had been there all along. His heart started to race despite his exhaustion. "I have to talk to her. I need to see her."

"Oh no you don't. I've booked you a separate room. There's no way in hell I'm going to let Lucia get any more involved with you than she already is before she knows the truth."

Ryan nodded and signaled to the waitress for the check. Much as he might hate the situation, he couldn't fault Lucia's friends for trying to protect her. So he would go back to their room. Alone.

Yup. Worst wedding night ever.

Chapter 10

Lucia woke up the next morning feeling like hell, groaning as the full force of her hangover hit her. Her head pounded, her mouth tasted like something had died in it, and her stomach churned. And then her brain started to wake up and memories of the night before came back with a vengeance.

Had she really...? *Gotten married? Yes, she had.*

And had she actually...? *Tried to seduce the man who married her for her money? Yup.*

Well done, Lucia.

Her next groan was met by Holly's disturbingly chipper voice. "Morning, sunshine."

Lucia opened one eye slowly and found that she was sprawled out on the couch in Holly and Jack's suite. Jack was already eating breakfast at the little table by the window and Holly was leaning over her with a steaming mug of coffee.

Thank God for coffee. What actually came out of her mouth was more of a mumbled groan than actual words.

"Sleep well?" Jack asked. Or rather, that's what she assumed he asked, his words were somewhat garbled as he chewed a bagel.

Lucia moved her feet so Holly could plop down beside her. Holly.... where had Holly gone last night? Turning to her friend, she was about to ask when Holly cut her off. "Uh-uh-uh. Your *husband* will be here in a bit and he can explain everything...including why we're here."

The word "husband" had a strange reaction on her insides. Part of her quivered in fear while the other part quivered in....something else. Excitement, maybe? Lust, definitely.

She stopped herself from groaning aloud again at the thought of how close she'd come to satisfaction the night before. Sure, she'd been drunk. And yes, sleeping with one's husband-of-convenience would probably muddy the waters a bit....but still. It would have been worth it to finally give in to a desire the likes of which she'd never come close to experiencing before.

Her sigh had Jack coming to sit on the loveseat beside her and Holly watching her with a concerned frown.

"Where's Ryan?" she asked, hoping to squelch any and all questions before they had a chance to start the interrogation.

"In his room." Was it her imagination or did Holly and Jack exchange *a look*.

"Okay, spill." She took another sip of her coffee and watched with some amusement as her friends had a silent sparring match over who was going to talk to her. Apparently Jack lost.

"We're not saying Ryan is a bad guy...." he started.

"Definitely not." Holly nodded for him to keep going as though she hadn't interrupted.

"But we don't think you know the whole story," Jack continued.

Nerves made her already queasy stomach a sloshing pit of acid. "What do you know?" She took a deep breath to try and calm her breathing. "I mean aside from the fact that we're married. What aren't you telling me about Ryan?"

They exchanged another look that had her wishing she could strangle them both. "Just tell me."

"Lucia," Holly started. She shared another look with Jack before ending, "Your new hubby is not what he seems."

Alarm bells went off. Like...literal alarm bells.

"Oh crap." Holly reached over to grab her phone and tapped something to turn off the alarm.

Before she could ask again, there was a knock at the door.

Ryan.

Jack sprang up to get the door before she could even move to set down her mug and she was glad she hadn't rushed. It wasn't Ryan.

It was *him*. The lowlife private detective her ex had hired to find her. Tracking her down and exposing her secrets hadn't been enough, evidently. Now the smug, squirrely looking man was in their doorway. With a little glance toward Lucia that put her last nerve on edge, she heard him mutter something to Jack, who nodded before closing the door.

"You're working with that guy now?" Lucia accused.

"No." Jack took back his seat beside her. "But when we needed to figure out where you were. He...helped." After a second he added, "For a price."

"Why did you need to find me?" Exasperation laced her voice. "I was fine. I knew what I was getting into. It was *my* idea."

He and Holly looked at each other again. One of those serious, we-know-each-other-so-well-we-don't-need-to-speak kinds of looks that drove her mad. "Why did you come after me? And why would you involve that...." She gestured after the man who had left, all English taking a temporary leave of absence thanks to her hung-over, frustrated state.

"Ryan can explain," Holly said. Then she winced a bit and added, "In Italy."

* * * *

"What?" Lucia sat upright too quickly and nearly spilled her coffee. She groaned in misery as her body protested the sudden movement. "What are you talking about, we're not going back. Not yet."

Jack's expression was filled with sympathy as he handed her a large glass of water. "You got married to gain access to your trust fund, right?"

Lucia nodded and then wished she hadn't. Her head was in an extremely fragile state. "Of course."

Holly stepped in, her face a mirror image of Jack's pitying look. "Sorry to break it to you, sweetie, but the trust fund stipulates that he has to sign off on it as long as you're under thirty."

"Wait....what?" The blood rushed from her head and left her tingling. This could not be happening. She'd gotten married, for God's sakes. And for what? For *nothing*? "That doesn't make sense," she said. "Grandpa never mentioned that rule."

Jack and Holly exchanged a look. "In his defense," Jack started. "He probably thought you'd marry someone he...."

Liked? Admired? Trusted? Lucia's brain filled in the blanks for him.

"Someone he'd met," he finished.

"Someone like Marco." Lucia glanced up at her friends whose silence was answer enough.

She fell back onto couch back with a sigh. "So now what?"

There was another knock on the door and Holly leapt up to answer.

Ryan. Nervous excitement warred with fear. That battle, combined with her nausea, was nearly enough to make her vomit. She swallowed thickly. How the hell was she going to explain this to Ryan? *Hi, thanks for marrying me. Turns out it was all for nothing. Just a silly misunderstanding.*

No way. She would have to tell him the truth. There was no money in this for him. She'd made a promise she couldn't keep. Maybe it was a good thing they hadn't shared a room together after all...the fact that they didn't consummate the marriage had to be good for an annulment case, right?

She heard the door opening and male voices but couldn't bring herself to face him. Not yet. This was the most humiliating thing that had happened to her but worse than that....tears pricked the back of her eyes at the thought that with this conversation, it would all be over. There would be no need to see one another ever again except maybe as employer and employee if she had the nerve to return to the hotel bar.

"What are you doing here?" Jack's voice cut through her emotional fog.

"That's harsh. He *is* my husband," Lucia muttered under her breath.

"Danny?" Holly was looking over Lucia's shoulder, her nose scrunched up in confusion. "What are you doing here?"

Lucia spun around and saw Daniel heading towards her, his forehead furrowed with concern.

"Daniel?"

Daniel sat across from her on the loveseat and rested his elbows on his knees. "This is all my fault, Lucia. I had to come and make sure you were all right."

Lucia's brain refused to comprehend. Was she supposed to understand that comment?

"Danny, what are you talking about?" Lucia hitched herself up so she was fully upright with her feet on the ground so she could face her overprotective—and clearly concerned—family friend.

Daniel sighed. "Ryan was using you to get to me."

The words were a punch in the gut but they made no sense. Still, adrenaline started coursing through her blood as an ominous sense of foreboding fell over her. What the hell was he talking about?

She was distantly aware of Holly muttering, "Way to be subtle, Danny."

Daniel shook his head in frustration. "I'm so sorry, Lucia, I should have seen this coming."

"Seen what coming?" The words came out of her frozen lips.

Daniel leaned forward, his hands clasped between his knees and his lips pressed together. Jack came to sit beside her and wrapped an arm around her shoulders in a brotherly move. Holly, she noted, was standing near the window behind Daniel, worrying her bottom lip.

This couldn't be good.

"Ryan's real last name is Brentworth." There was a tense silence in the room after Daniel's pronouncement and Lucia fought a nervous giggle. She'd never been good with tense silences and Daniel's big news was so...anti-climactic.

"I know," she said.

Daniel glanced back at Holly over his shoulder and she mouthed. "You're too late."

"They got married last night," Jack added.

Lucia drew in a deep breath. She loved her friends but this kind of over-protectiveness was the very reason she'd left Italy. It was why she hadn't told anyone about her plans.

"Look, I appreciate your concern. But I know Ryan's real name and I know why he lied."

Her friends exchanged glances. "You do?" Holly asked.

Lucia rolled her eyes. "Yes, and it's not that big of a deal."

Daniel leaned back in his seat, his eyes narrowed as he studied her. She'd seen Daniel at work often enough to know that look—it meant his mind was whirring, putting the pieces together.

Jack and Holly seemed to be waiting for him to speak. Or maybe they were waiting for her. Either way they were watching her and Daniel with an intensity that was unnerving.

"So," Daniel started. "He told you that my company bought out his family's business?"

Lucia blinked at him. Her heart rate picked up speed and her stomach, which was already a roiling mess, threatened to toss its contents all over the rug.

"What?" Lucia's voice was little more than a whisper but she knew they'd heard her because all three seemed to deflate with disappointment.

She cleared her throat. "What are you talking about?"

Lucia was distantly aware of a light knock on the door. Holly went to answer it as Daniel started to explain. "About ten years ago I learned of the Brentworth's financial difficulties." Before he could get any further, they were distracted by Ryan's voice coming from the doorway.

"Luce, I can explain."

Daniel and Jack shot up at once but Lucia was frozen on the couch. A thousand weights seemed to be pressing down on her, holding her in place.

"You can explain?" Jack growled.

Daniel's voice was clipped and cold. "You've done enough harm here, Mr. Brentworth. My lawyers are already drawing up a restraining order. I suggest you—"

Holly held up a hand to stop him. "Daniel, enough. I promised Ryan he would be the one to explain."

Lucia was only vaguely aware of the bickering that broke out between Holly, Jack, and Daniel as they debated whether to let Ryan into the room, let alone give him a chance to speak. Lucia was too distracted by

Ryan—her husband. He was still standing in the doorway but he'd met her gaze the moment he'd walked through the door and hadn't broken eye contact since.

He seemed content to stand there and await the verdict of her friends.

Lucia wished she could read something in those eyes—guilt, or even better, anger at these false accusations. But she couldn't read anything there other than what she'd always seen when she'd looked into those gorgeous blues—a kindness that warmed her to her core.

"Can you guys give us a minute?"

Her friends turned to her in surprise. Jack and Daniel were both scowling but Holly gave her a small, encouraging smile.

"Are you sure?" Jack asked.

"We're not leaving you alone in this room with *him*," Daniel said at the same time.

The shock and hurt that had kept her frozen on the couch lifted, thanks to Daniel's commanding tone. If there was one thing she hated it was being told what to do.

Tossing her hair over her shoulder and lifting her chin, she stood up straight and tried to look as dignified as possible—which was probably not all that dignified given her hung-over state.

"Fine," she said, moving past her friends to the doorway where Ryan still stood watching her. "Then I guess we'll go to *our* room."

She ignored the protests as she walked out the door, not looking back to see if Ryan was following her.

* * * *

Ryan followed his new bride down the hall to the elevator. *Who was this woman and how had he managed to make her his wife?* That was all he could think as he stood beside her for the short ride to their floor.

She was still wearing the short, flimsy black dress from the night before and her long black hair was tousled. Her heels dangled from her hand as she padded barefoot down the hallway. She looked like a woman doing the walk of shame....and it was goddamn sexy.

This was not the time to be ogling his wife. She'd been silent since they left the room and now, as they keyed into the room they shared, he found himself at a loss for words. He should be preparing what he was going to say, not staring at her like some sex-starved teen.

Once inside, she dropped her heels, and stopped in front of her overnight bag. She glanced over her shoulder at him, confusion in her eyes.

"I couldn't sleep last night so I gathered our belongings from the motel and checked us out."

Lucia just nodded and headed toward the bag.

"Lucia, I need you to know—"

She held up a hand to stop him and started digging through her bag. She pulled out a makeup bag and walked past him. "I can't talk yet. Give me a minute."

She went into the bathroom and locked the door, leaving Ryan to sit on the edge of the bed and wait. He heard water running and his anxiety increased exponentially with every minute that ticked by.

This was it. This was his one chance to make things right with this woman or she could disappear from his life. Forever.

That thought was terrifying. Fear gripped him and made his chest feel like it was locked in a vice. He couldn't let that happen. He couldn't lose her. Not when he'd just found her.

Holy hell, at what point had he started to care so deeply? Ryan thrust a hand through his hair. This was no crush. It wasn't even pure lust. This was something more. Something so much deeper. Somehow over the course of the past week, he'd come to need this woman in his life as surely as he needed oxygen.

And he had no idea if she felt the same way. Even if she'd felt a connection too—all that could be gone now that she knew the truth about him.

He heard the water shut off in the bathroom. She'd come out any minute now and he would need to explain himself and his actions.

He would tell her everything. A vague sense of guilt gnawed at his stomach at thought of revealing his family secrets but anger squashed that guilt and filled him with rage. He was furious with his family—with his brother for his ridiculous schemes and his constant jabs at Ryan for not doing enough to vindicate their father. And he was just as angry with his mother for continuing to bait him and fuel Billy's anger.

Even his father, who he'd adored as a kid—he was even angry with him for losing the family business in the first place and, worse, for leaving them. Everyone said the overdose was accidental but he'd never known if that was the truth. Whether it was accidental or not, his father had given up the battle with booze long before his death. Even as a kid, he'd known that.

The bathroom door clicked open and Lucia stepped out, still wearing that dress but her face was scrubbed of last night's makeup and her hair was tied back in a ponytail that made her look even younger than her twenty-four years.

Still barefoot, Lucia stood before him in the middle of the room and shifted her weight from one foot to the other as her hands toyed with the makeup bag in her hands. She looked so sweet and innocent. It was all he could do not to sweep her up into his arms and promise to protect her, take care of her, and keep her from harm.

But so far, he was the only one who had harmed her. *He'd* hurt her.

"I was an idiot." He hadn't actually meant to say it out loud. In fact, he'd had a whole speech planned out, but those were the words that came out. Her eyes widened in surprise and he realized it was as good a place as any to start. Because it was the truth.

"I was an idiot," he said again, "because I honestly thought that I could do this...." He made a broad sweeping gesture. "I thought I could make things right for my family without involving you. Without *hurting* you."

Lucia tossed the bag on a nightstand and crossed her arms in front of her. She wasn't looking at him now and the only indication she'd heard him was the slight wrinkle of her brow.

"So it's true?" She was so quiet, so serene, so....not like the little Italian spitfire he'd come to know. His heart twisted in his chest.

"Yes."

She gave a little nod as her eyes continued to focus on everything but him. He heard her mutter something but couldn't make it out.

"What did you say?"

She looked up, her eyes were wet with unshed tears. Guilt and regret sliced through his gut like a sword.

"I said, *I* am the idiot." *For believing you.* She didn't say the words, but she didn't have to. He heard the accusation there.

"I didn't mean to involve you in this," he started. But he was well aware how lame that sounded.

Lucia's lips twitched up in a small, sad smile. "All right then, how about you tell me what you did mean to do."

Ryan took a deep breath. This was his chance to explain, to make everything right. But where to start? "My family....my mother and my brother, that is...they blame Daniel for our situation."

"And what situation is that?" Lucia's foot tapped against the rug and her mouth was set in a firm line.

He cleared his throat. "Uh, you see, we used to be rich. Very, very rich."

Lucia raised her brows. "And?"

Ryan opened his mouth and then shut it again. What was the point of rehashing his family's past? None of that mattered anymore. Some of the weight on his chest lifted at that thought. For the first time in years he realized that he didn't need to be anchored down by his family's past. His mother and brother's battles didn't have to be his. He could say goodbye to the past and move on.

A rush of energy jolted through him and for the first time since God knows when, he could see a future that wasn't bleak and depressing. He could see a future with Lucia.

Moving forward he took her hands in his and ignored her gasp of surprise. "I need you to listen to me, Lucia. I didn't want to drag you into the middle of my family's feud with Daniel."

Her eyes widened but she didn't respond.

"Yes, I wanted to use the money we got to appease my family. And yes, I was hoping to anger Daniel Gladwell in the process." He shook his head at his own stupidity. "I don't even know what I was planning to do… make some baseless threats, maybe, or blackmail him…."

Her expression turned from surprise to horror and he stopped himself. "It doesn't matter. I didn't think it through because part of me already knew that I wouldn't go through with it. It was never about you, Lucia, it was about getting even with Daniel. And getting revenge isn't worth it if it means hurting you."

He stopped to catch his breath and marveled at the lightness he felt as the words coming out of his mouth rang true. He didn't know when it had happened or how, but the joy that Lucia brought into his life now outweighed the bitter need for payback. This woman—his wife—had somehow managed to shed light on that dark part of his life. The bleakness of the past was nothing in comparison to the brightness of his future. But that bright future depended on her forgiving him.

Lucia tugged her hands from his. She turned and walked to the window and stood there with her back to him. She was silent for a couple of minutes but it seemed like hours. His brain was coming up with more excuses, more rationalizations…more ways to make her see that he was sorry. Then, like the idiot he was, he realized that for the second time in their brief relationship, he had failed to do the obvious.

"I'm sorry." His words sounded loud in the quiet room.

She was still looking out the window but he heard a noise. He couldn't tell if it was a soft laugh, a sad sigh, or the telltale sniffle of tears. He willed her to turn around—to let him know that she was all right and she could forgive him.

Finally she spoke, while still facing the window. "Do you know why I hate being called princess?"

He shook his head and then realized she couldn't see him. "Why?"

"Because it's what my grandfather used to call me when I was little. At that point, I hadn't learned the truth about my absent father and I actually believed that he was royalty. I was little and stupid and didn't realize that it was just an endearment."

She laughed, but the sound was so sad and tired, it made his fists clench at his side. He would do anything to take away that pain.

Turning from the window, she moved to the chair across from him and sank into it with a sigh. "You see, my mother was just like me. She was naïve and stupid and, by all accounts, a bit of a wild child." Lucia's eyes were unfocused. Ryan stayed still on the bed across from her, unwilling to interrupt. He was getting a glimpse of the real Lucia—it was the kind of honesty and openness he didn't expect from her. And he certainly didn't deserve it.

"Grandpa openly admits that he spoiled her. He gave her everything she wanted, even the cross-country trip in America when she graduated high school, despite the fact that she'd hardly ever left our small town and was sheltered and innocent."

Lucia met his gaze then and gave her head a little shake as if to bring herself back to the moment. "Anyway, long story short. She thought she'd found love, and I was conceived."

"And it wasn't love?" Ryan guessed.

Lucia rolled her eyes. "She thought it was. Right up until Grandpa offered the guy money to walk away. And he took it."

Ryan stifled a groan and resisted the urge to reach out to her. She must have seen the sympathy in his eyes because she stiffened. "It's all right. I never even met the man so it means nothing to me."

That was a lie and he knew it but he let it go.

She flashed him a smile then but it was not the genuine warm grin he was used to. It was cold and knowing. Her eyes held more than a little bitterness. "So you see…being duped by gold diggers runs in the family."

Ouch. Ryan's head jerked back as if he'd been slapped. He stood and moved so he was directly in front of her. "I deserve that."

Her false smile flickered before fading. He grabbed her hands and tugged until she was standing before him. He framed her face in his hands and tried to focus his thoughts. He had to make this right before he lost her forever.

He looked into her eyes, hoping she could see everything he was feeling, everything he was incapable of putting into words. "I didn't mean to use you, Luce. That's why I turned you down the first time you asked. But then I realized that this could be my chance to end my family's vendetta and move on with all of our lives."

He could see her swallow and her eyes brimmed with tears. "I guess it's hypocritical of me, huh?" Her voice was so low, he dropped his hands from her face but moved closer so he could hear every word.

"What do you mean?"

She swiped at her eyes before looking back up at him. "I mean, we were both using each other for money. I can't really blame you for that."

The fear that had been eating him alive started to ease a bit. "I'm not blameless here," he felt compelled to add.

She nodded. "I know."

"But I promise I never intended to hurt you in all of this." A heavy silence hung in the air as he waited for her to respond as though his life hung in the balance. And maybe it did. His happiness was at stake, at the very least.

"You already did."

The honest heartbreak in her eyes was his undoing. "I don't want any of it," he said. And as the words came out of his mouth he realized how true they were. She blinked up at him in confusion.

"I don't want the money or the revenge," he continued. "I don't want any of it. Not if it means losing you."

Chapter 11

Lucia's heart threatened to burst from her chest. He would give up all that money and the chance to get revenge....for her?

It didn't make what he'd done okay but it did ease the hurt so it was no longer a searing pain. Now there was just a dull throb wherever her pride was located.

Don't be a fool, Lucia, these are just words.

"Why would you do that?" she asked.

He opened his mouth and no words came out. She saw the understanding dawn. It was like watching a light flicker on in those beautiful eyes of his. But he still hadn't answered so she pressed again. "Why would you do that? Why would you give it all up?"

His words came out on a rush of air. "Because I care about you and I think I...I think I'm falling for you."

Lucia stopped breathing. She stopped moving. She was fairly certain her pulse even took a momentary pause before picking up its pace.

He didn't mean it. He couldn't. But then she looked into his eyes and saw the genuine emotions there. She nearly drowned in the sheer joy that exploded inside of her. His words had unlocked a desire she hadn't even let herself acknowledge. She liked him. She cared about him...and he felt the same way. The breath she'd been holding came out in a ragged laugh. "That's...that's crazy."

Ryan looked as stricken by the words as she was and he started to laugh too. "I know. But I can't help it." He gave her a helpless shrug that had her laughing even harder.

She stopped as soon as he reached out to her. Wrapping his arms around her he pulled her up against him and all laughter stopped as Lucia struggled to breathe normally. Her brain was a scattered mess and her body...well her body was on fire.

"Lucia Antoinette Brunell," he started.

"That's still not my middle name," she interjected.

"Whatever. Lucia Brunelli, you are the best thing to come into my life since....well, ever. I know I don't deserve a second chance but I don't want to lose you so if you'll just—"

Lucia couldn't take any more. She thought she might melt right then and there in his arms. So she kissed him, mid-sentence. His lips clung to hers after his initial surprise and then his hands were tangled in her hair, holding her to him as her arms wrapped around his waist. He pulled back briefly. "Lucia, I swear, I will never hurt you—"

She cut him off with another kiss. "Save the speeches for later."

Her heart did a little flip as he gave her one of his sexy smiles and leaned in to kiss her again, this time with a tenderness that was heart-achingly sweet. His lips teased hers as his hands moved from her hair to her neck, and then down her back so he could press the length of her body against his.

She let out a soft moan as her curves pressed up against his hard chest. His lips trailed down her neck, finding the sensitive spot beneath her earlobe that made her gasp.

Her fingers fumbled with the buttons on his shirt. She needed to touch him and feel the heat of his skin against hers. He helped her in between kisses and soon his shirt was on the floor and her hands were running over his chest and the taut muscles of his stomach. But she wanted more. She needed more.

His hands were everywhere, leaving a trail of heat wherever they roamed. From her back to her waist, to her hips and backside. Her dress was thin and she could feel his warmth but it wasn't enough. She needed to be closer. Her mind was a cloudy fog of desperation as she clung to him. He groaned against her lips as her hands inched lower, getting dangerously close to the button of his jeans.

He kissed her fiercely, his tongue claiming her mouth and his hands grasping her ass and pressing her up against him so she could feel his desire. Slipping his fingers beneath the hem of her dress, he paused just long enough to give her time to protest. Instead, she whispered, "Yes."

There was no turning back now and she couldn't even if she tried. Her body had a mind of its own and it was in control. And it wanted this. *She* wanted this.

He slipped the dress over her head in one quick move and he took a small step back to look at her, clad only in a lacy black bra and panties. Lucia struggled to stay in place and not throw herself against him as his eyes moved over her, dark with desire and with a look of hunger that drove her wild.

"You're gorgeous." The words came out as a deep, throaty growl before he pulled her back against him, his hands moving over her stomach to her breasts, which were straining against the thin material of the bra. She was all but panting with desire when his finger flicked over her hard nipples, teasing her through the thin lace.

Her fingers fumbled with the button of his jeans before he stilled her hands with his. She pulled back in surprise. Why was he stopping?

But then he leaned over so he could scoop her into his arms and placed her gently on the bed. She watched with breathless fascination as he unfastened his jeans and slid them off, along with his underwear so he was standing before her, perfectly nude and intimidatingly hot.

Then he moved over her, kneeling beside her on the bed so he could kiss her lips and her neck and then her breasts, licking at her nipple through the lace and sending shivers through her. His hands continued their assault, roaming over every inch of her, sliding over her thighs and hips, pausing just before he reached her core, which was wet and aching to be touched.

"Please," she whispered.

That word seemed to snap whatever restraint he had left. Moving quickly he unfastened her bra, slipped off her panties, and lowered himself on top of her so she could feel the warm, hard weight of him between her thighs.

She moved to meet him, tilting her hips to give him full access and when he drove inside of her, her head tilted back and her back arched at the sheer, exquisite pleasure. His lips never left hers as he moved inside her, the tension building with every thrust, every touch, every sigh.

Her fingers dug into his back and she cried out his name when she tumbled over the edge of reason and her body shattered into a million pieces. She heard him growl her name as he came right after.

* * * *

She could have stayed like that for hours. Snuggled against Ryan's side, she listened to his heartbeat beneath her ear. Maybe it *had* been hours. Apparently amazing sex had a direct effect on her ability to gauge time. Who knew? Certainly not her. Sex with Marco had never been like this. It was always…pleasant. A nice pastime for a nice couple.

It had never been earthshattering. Mind-blowing. She'd never lost all reason or forgotten her own name. She let out a little sigh. *This* she could get used to.

Ryan shifted beneath her at the sound of her sigh. "Everything okay?" he murmured into her hair.

Lucia nodded. "Perfect."

One of his hands lazily trailed up and down her side. "*You're* perfect."

She had to laugh at that. "Not exactly. But it was a pretty perfect wedding."

"I'm so sorry, Luce. For everything."

She studied his eyes and saw the guilt, the regret. "No more apologies. That's in the past. But from here on out, we're honest with each other. About everything. Deal?"

"Deal." He gave her a light kiss before pulling back again. "And I meant what I said earlier. We can go get this wedding annulled this morning. Start fresh."

Lucia stroked the five o'clock shadow that was starting to appear as she thought through her options. She knew he meant it. He would give up millions just to be with her. He would even put her and this…relationship? Was it really a relationship? Overwhelming joy threatened to take over.

Focus. There will be plenty of time for girly squealing after you figure out what to do next.

He would put their relationship before his mother and brother. That was huge. And…maybe that was enough.

Ryan propped himself up on one elbow so he was looking down at her. "What do you say? Let's file for an annulment and then I'll take you out on a proper date." He paused. "That sounded more romantic in my head."

Lucia laughed. "Maybe we should put that annulment on hold for a bit."

Ryan's brows shot up. "Oh yeah? You're enjoying this whole married lady thing, huh?"

She gave his shoulder a playful shove. "No, I just think…maybe we shouldn't call off the original plan."

He looked like he was about to protest but Lucia cut him off. "I mean, yes, you should have told me the whole truth about your family and your plans, but—does that really mean we have to throw away all of our plans?"

When he gave her a blank look, she continued on in a rush. "I mean, sure we would have to fly to Italy and convince my grandfather but we've come this far, why not see it through?"

She sat up, grabbing a nearby sheet to cover herself, suddenly modest now that they were back on earth and talking about something as unromantic as fooling her grandfather.

Ryan fell back against the pillows and studied her with a wary look. "I don't know, Lucia. Daniel will never go for it—"

Lucia rolled her eyes. "Let me handle Daniel."

Ryan frowned. "Lucia, I don't want the money. I don't need the revenge."

"Yeah, but I do," she said. At his wide-eyed look of surprise, she added. "I mean, not the revenge. But I still want the money. It's mine and I'm entitled to it. I don't want to wait six years before I have my shot at a fashion line of my own just because my family has antiquated views on marriage and money."

"I don't know," Ryan said.

Lucia was on a roll. "And your family deserves that money. From everything you told me, it would help them come to peace with whatever happened between Daniel and your father. And maybe it would help them get over their...." She threw her hands up, at a loss for the word.

"Bitterness?" Ryan supplied. "Resentment? All-consuming anger?"

"Exactly." Lucia beamed at him. "Everybody wins."

Ryan's eyes narrowed as he studied her and she could practically see his mind at work. "If this is really what you want..."

"It is." And it was. The more she thought it through, the more it made sense. They'd already come this far. They were married, for heaven's sake. Why throw it all away?

"Okay then," Ryan said, tugging her arm until she was sprawled across his chest. "Annulment postponed. I guess this means we'll be married for a little while longer." His hands slipped beneath the sheet and over her hip. "However shall we spend our honeymoon?"

* * * *

In Lucia's opinion, their honeymoon was perfection.

True to her word, she'd handled Daniel. Well, handled probably wasn't the best word for it. She'd basically called to let him know they wouldn't be able to fly out for a couple of days, hung up, and then refused to answer any of his calls. Childish? Perhaps. But it wasn't every day one's new husband declared he was falling for her and Lucia meant to enjoy every damn second of her honeymoon.

And oh, what a honeymoon.

"I'm not moving." Ryan was curled up around her; the big spoon as he called it. She turned her head so she could see him over her shoulder. Lord, he was cute when he was sleepy.

"We haven't moved for two days," Lucia said with a laugh. And she wasn't exaggerating. The only times they'd left the bed was to use the bathroom, shower, or answer the door for room service. She didn't want to move either but today was the day. Daniel's plane was ready and waiting to take them to Italy. To see her grandfather.

Right. No need to panic.

"Hey, you okay?" Ryan shifted them so he was looking down at her.

She forced a smile for his sake. They'd been over this. He was on board to sell this relationship to her grandfather. They were in the home stretch. The money was almost hers. All she had to do was face her grandfather.

"I don't want the honeymoon to end," she admitted with a sigh.

He leaned down to nuzzle her neck. "Me neither." *And we don't have to.*

He didn't say it but he didn't have to. Ryan had mentioned more than once during their talks that he'd be fine walking away from the money. Maybe he was fine with it, but she was not. She was the first to admit she was stubborn and this was something she wasn't willing to budge on.

Ryan's lips had moved from her neck to her shoulder and Lucia's muscles turned to putty. How did he do it? It was like he knew every trigger and switch in her body.

A sigh of contentment slipped out as he pulled her against him, the lengths of their bodies pressed together.

"What's that sigh about?"

Lucia kept her eyes closed but she grinned. "Who would have thought getting married would land me a boyfriend?"

She felt the rumble of his low laughter in his chest and opened her eyes to see him smiling down at her. "Is that what I am now? Your *boyfriend*? I'm pretty sure I was just demoted."

Lucia laughed. She'd been laughing a lot these past two days—more than she could ever remember. "Not demoted," she argued. "You are my fake husband but my real boyfriend."

He pretended to mull it over before leaning down to plant a kiss on her lips. "Fair enough."

A wave of excitement rippled through her leaving her breathless in a way that was starting to feel familiar. Is this what it felt like to fall in love?

Neither of them had actually used the L-word yet but it was there between them, waiting to be claimed. Although he had said he was falling for her…was that the same thing?

Not so fast. Her inner voice of reason told her to take it slow.

But taking it slow was kind of hard to do when you're already married.

That thought had her giggling again as Ryan trailed kisses over her cheeks and eyelids. "What's so funny?"

Lucia gave a little shake of her head. "Nothing. Everything…. Us."

He started laughing as well. "I guess this isn't the most typical start to a relationship, huh?"

She shook her head. "Typical is boring."

When he leaned back in for more kisses, she gently pushed him away with a pout. "I hate to say it, but it's time we leave this bed. Daniel will blow a fuse if we miss the flight."

"Blow a fuse" was a new phrase she'd learned from Ryan and she thought it was very fitting...especially for Daniel.

Ryan pulled back and tucked a lock of hair behind her ear. His obvious disappointment was adorable. Okay fine, so maybe she thought everything Ryan did was pretty cute. She couldn't help it—he was irresistible.

"Are you saying the honeymoon's over?" he asked. She raised one brow and he caved. "I know, I know. We need to face reality eventually."

Ugh. Reality. Lucia pulled the covers up around her instinctively and Ryan buried his face in her neck. The bed was a blissful safe haven. But out there?

"Have you told your family about me yet?" she asked.

She felt his nod against her neck.

"Even my connection to Daniel?"

He nodded again. "I told them the plan."

She inhaled deeply trying to summon the courage to get out of the bed. "Good." While it wasn't exactly romantic knowing her new boyfriend's mother and brother were eager to use her for her money, she was glad it was out in the open. They'd spent a good portion of the last two days talking—among other things—and it was a relief they were both on the same page. Now they just had to make sure their families fell in line.

He pulled back enough to look her in the eyes. "They know that you are off limits," he assured her. "I made it clear, we're dropping the revenge part of this plan."

"And they're okay with that?"

He gave a little half shrug. "They have to be. I told them it was either revenge or the money."

She stroked back the hair falling into his face and tried not to show how much her heart ached on his behalf. She couldn't imagine growing up in a family that was filled with such hate. Now her family on the other hand....

"I wish I could fast forward through this whole talk with my grandfather. He's just such a romantic, he's never going to understand." Before he could rush to reassure her for the hundredth time, she added, "I think you're going to like Grandpa. Everyone does."

Because he was the best. Which was why it was ridiculous that she was so nervous to face him. But that was family for you. No one else's opinions mattered half so much.

"It's not him I'm worried about."

"You think *he* won't like *you*?" she asked. "Impossible! He'll love you. You're the most likeable man I know."

He turned his head to kiss her palm and flashed her a wicked grin. "Why, thank you, my sweet. But that wasn't what I meant."

At her blank expression, he said, "I'm not sure I'll be alive long enough to meet your grandfather. I've seen the texts you've been getting from Daniel and heard his voicemails, remember?" He fell back against the pillows with a groan. "You may have to explain this marriage to your grandfather but at least you don't have to get on a plane with a man who hates you."

Lucia couldn't argue with that.

* * * *

Daniel was the only other passenger on the plane aside from him and Lucia. Of course Daniel had to be there since it was his plane and all. But still. Ryan didn't think he could take many more hours of being cooped up in a small room with a man who only looked up from his laptop to glare at him. Despite Lucia's sweet-talking and promises that Daniel would let bygones be bygones, his glare promised a slow and torturous death, if Daniel had his way.

But somehow Lucia had managed to convince him to take them to Italy on his jet, as her grandfather had requested, so that they could prove to him that their love was real.

Love. Who would have guessed that he would fall in love with his wife?

His choked laugh caught Lucia's attention. She looked up from her book. "You doing okay?"

Ryan nodded and took a sip of the bottled water the flight attendant had given him. "Fine. Just checking to make sure the water isn't poisoned."

Lucia laughed. "I promise, Daniel will leave you alone."

"Mmm-hmmm."

Lucia laughed again at his sarcastic tone. "I swear. Daniel promised to be on his best behavior and he always keeps his promises."

Ryan took another sip of water rather than answer. He may have put his family's plans for vengeance to the side for Lucia's sake but he didn't really want to hear yet again what a great and honorable man Daniel was.

Daniel chose that moment to look up from his laptop and skewer Ryan with another cold, steely glare. When he dropped his gaze back to his laptop, Ryan whispered, "See?"

He turned to see Lucia smothering a laugh. "Don't pay attention to him. He'll get over it." He raised an eyebrow and she added, "Eventually."

"Yeah, at my funeral, maybe." He muttered under his breath so only Lucia could hear but her giggle had Daniel glaring his way again.

"Seriously," she said. "He will. He's just worried about me." She flashed him an adorable grin. "Ivy says worry is Daniel's default setting—it's how he shows he cares."

"Poor Ivy," he said with a laugh.

Lucia nodded. "Poor Baby Anna. Daniel is going to be one overprotective father." She said it with a little sigh and Ryan knew exactly what she was thinking.

Daniel would be the kind of father she never had. What kind of man would walk away from his daughter for money?

What kind of father would abandon his family for lack of money? He shook off that thought. It wasn't fair to blame his father who wasn't here to defend himself.

"Tell me again, how is this going to work?" he asked, wrapping an arm around Lucia and pulling her close to his side. He still couldn't believe she was trusting him and giving him a second chance. Lord knows, he wouldn't have done the same thing if he were in her shoes. Hell, he'd practically bitten her head off when he'd found out there was more to her than she'd let on.

Maybe he didn't deserve the second chance, but he'd be damned if he wasn't going to take it. Not only that, he would use this opportunity to help her get everything she wanted in life—everything she deserved. And if that meant fooling an old man so she could launch her career, he was all in.

Lucia sighed, the only sign she wasn't quite as okay with this plan as she kept insisting. "It's simple, really. We just have to convince my grandfather that we're in love."

"That shouldn't be too hard," Ryan whispered.

She gave him a considering look that made him smile. "It's not that I doubt your acting abilities," she started.

"Who says I'd be acting?"

"It's just…my grandfather…well, he might be the world's biggest romantic. He's going to hate the fact that I married for money."

"Wait. Hold up. I thought the whole point of this trip to Italy was to make your grandfather believe we married for love."

Lucia turned in her seat so she was facing him directly. "Oh please. My grandfather is a romantic, not an idiot. He knows I need money and there's no way we'd fool him into thinking this marriage was only about love."

"Okaaay," Ryan drawled. "Then what's our story?"

Lucia said with a shrug, "We'll keep it simple. We became friends and decided to marry for money, but somewhere along the way, we...." She bit her lip for a moment before finishing, "Somewhere along the way we...developed feelings."

Developed feelings? Not exactly the most romantic way of putting it but he supposed it was accurate enough. "So we stick with the truth, then." Ryan found himself holding his breath waiting for her to answer. He was acutely aware of the fact that while he had told her he was falling for her, she had yet to reciprocate.

Oh, she'd admitted she'd liked him. She'd even gone so far as to tell him she'd developed a crush at first sight. And she'd referred to him as her boyfriend today—that had to be a good sign, right? But the L-word had never been spoken. And now? He exhaled loudly. Now she still hadn't admitted she was falling for him too. Lucia's smile was unreadable as she kept talking, ignoring the giant "I'm falling for you"-sized elephant in the airplane. Well, what had he expected? He still had a ways to go before he earned her trust. But he would.

* * * *

The villa was nothing like he'd imagined. Not that he had much experience with Tuscan villas or Italy at all, for that matter. But from what little he knew, he hadn't expected it to be so....noisy.

There were children everywhere, along with aunts, uncles, friends of the family—including Ivy and Daniel's baby—and even some members of Daniel's family, who lived nearby.

And they were all there to meet him.

"Right, no pressure," Ryan said to Lucia as he helped her out of the car and into the mob scene that was her family.

Everyone was nice to him. *Too* nice to him. Particularly her grandfather. From the moment Ryan entered their home, he was welcomed with open arms by the patriarch, a jovial, gray-haired man with a loud laugh and eyes that seemed to see everything.

Only Daniel continued to treat him like a bug that had crawled out from under a rock, even when they all sat down to dinner. Ryan noticed that Daniel's wife elbowed him in the ribs every time he glared. By the end of dinner, Ryan was fairly certain Daniel was black and blue beneath his stiff-collared buttoned-down shirt. At least he had Ivy on his side.

It wasn't until after dinner that Lucia's grandfather asked to speak to him alone in his study. Ryan looked to Lucia who was helping to clear the dinner plates. She gave him a wink and mouthed, "Good luck."

He needed more than luck. He followed the older man down several hallways before they entered a dark, wood-paneled room that housed a large desk which was overflowing with papers.

Something told him, if this man didn't like him or believe their story… he would be on the next plane back to New York before he could say *ciao*. Brunelli waited until Ryan was seated in the chair opposite him at the desk.

The old man dispensed with the typical small talk, all of which had been covered over dinner anyways. He launched right into his attack. "What are your intentions toward my granddaughter?"

Ryan cleared his throat. "I would think it's fairly obvious, sir, seeing that I've married her."

Brunelli did not look amused. Ryan tried again. "I can understand your concern, sir. But believe me when I say—"

"That's the problem, Ryan. I don't believe you. I don't know what sort of game you and Lucia are up to but it ends here. It ends now."

Ryan shifted in his seat. He didn't want to argue with Lucia's grandfather but he couldn't just sit here and take it. "If you'll excuse me, sir, I think that's up to us."

"You're only in it for the money." Brunelli's jaw was clenched so tightly Ryan feared the old man might have a stroke.

"Yes, sir."

Brunelli blinked in confusion. "You're not even going to try to deny it?"

Ryan resisted the urge to laugh. Maybe her plan to tell the truth hadn't been so crazy after all. "No, sir. The intention was never to try and trick you into believing this was solely a love match."

Brunelli's eyes narrowed at his careful wording. "But it is a love match."

Ryan hesitated for only a second before he nodded. For him it was, at least. There was no use denying it. He was head over heels…for his wife.

Brunelli was quiet for a moment. "You met my little girl, what? A few weeks ago?"

"A little over a month ago," Ryan corrected.

Brunelli leaned back in his chair with a sigh. "You seem like a nice enough man and it's clear Lucia cares about you…"

Ryan actually found himself perking up at that. He resisted the urge to ask, "You really think so?" Now was not the time. But still it was good to hear.

"You have to understand. Lucia…she has been protected her whole life." Brunelli shrugged, "Maybe too much so. I didn't want to repeat the mistakes I made with her mother and…." For a moment, Ryan was certain Brunelli didn't even know he was there, he was too caught up in memories.

When Brunelli's eyes grew sad, Ryan started to feel sorry for him. But then he seemed to shake it off and he once again focused his laser-like attention on Ryan. "You barely know my granddaughter and she is everything to me. She is *mi principessa.* I'll do whatever it takes to protect her, even if it's from herself."

Ryan actually flinched at the nickname. "I know Lucia well enough to know she hates being called princess."

Brunelli's eyebrows shot up at that. But Ryan wasn't finished.

"She's also not a little girl any longer and while you may still want to protect her, it's well past time you consider what *she* wants."

Brunelli's mouth opened to protest, his wrinkled face filled with anger.

Ryan shifted forward in his seat. "Look, I'm not going to lie. The money would be nice. But that's not why I'm here. I would be here with or without the money."

Brunelli's expression was full of cynicism. "Then why are you here?"

Now it was Ryan's turn to study her grandfather. "Lucia once told me that you are the biggest romantic she's ever met. You should be able to figure it out."

Eyes wide, her grandfather let out a laugh. When Ryan made a move to leave, Brunelli stopped him.

"Ryan..." Her grandfather suddenly looked old and weary. "I just want her to be happy."

Ryan leaned forward. "Then give her what she wants."

"And what is that?"

"Her freedom," Ryan said. "She told me what happened with her mother and I can't imagine how painful that was. But Lucia deserves the chance to make her own decisions and to make her own way in this world."

He stood then, ready to head back out to find his wife, but he stopped to add, "Lucia may be the bravest, strongest, kindest, most amazing woman I've ever met. I know you love her, but I think it's time you trust her."

Chapter 12

That was, without a doubt, the sexiest thing Lucia had ever heard. Back pressed against the wall outside her grandfather's study, she'd heard every last word. Her grandfather never did seem to notice how much sound carried in the villa's cavernous hallway.

"What are you doing out here?" Ivy asked as she rounded the corner, Baby Anna balanced on her hip.

Lucia shushed her with a finger over her lips before dragging Ivy along with her down the hall to the library. Once inside she shut the door and turned to face her friend who was grinning at her. "What's with all the secrecy?"

Lucia shrugged, feigning nonchalance. "There's no secrecy."

"Uh huh. So, you weren't eavesdropping back there?"

Falling back into an overstuffed chair, Lucia laughed. "Okay, maybe I was being a little sneaky."

"Afraid your grandfather isn't going to believe you two are in love?"

Before Lucia could respond, her friend continued, "You have nothing to worry about. The way you two look at each other? It's obvious to everyone how you feel about one another."

A flicker of joy shot through her. "It is?"

It was?

Ivy's nod was decisive. "Absolutely. You guys are so clearly in love. It's pretty cute, actually."

Lucia ignored Ivy's smug smile; she was too distracted by the mixed emotions her words had churned up. The initial jolt of joy at hearing that Ryan loved her was followed by a rising sense of panic.

She hadn't said she was in love. Sure, there had been a couple of times when she thought that might be what this crazy, scary, out of control falling feeling was, but it wasn't official.

Not for her, at least.

She wasn't ready.

Lucia shook her head to rid herself of the thought. Relax. There was no need to panic. Ryan wasn't rushing her into anything—her friends and family just believed what she and Ryan expected them to.

Ivy's eyes narrowed on her when she failed to respond with a laugh or a quip. "What's wrong?"

Ugh. Her friend knew her too well.

Lucia forced a smile. "Nothing. Nothing at all."

Ivy cocked her head to the side and seemed to consider her, seemingly unaware her daughter was threatening to pull out a clump of her hair at any second. "You've got the look," she said before bursting into a grin that was the spitting image of her daughter's.

"I don't know what you're talking about."

Ivy gave an unladylike snort of disbelief. "Oh girl, I know that look. I *had* that look. And it's the same exact look Holly had when she showed up here looking for Jack."

Oh no. Don't say it.

"You're definitely in love," Ivy said. "And you're terrified."

"Am not." Okay, so maybe that had come out a bit more angsty-teen than intended. But she wasn't scared. She was never scared. With that thought she tipped her chin up. "I'm not afraid, I just…we just…we haven't defined the relationship."

She'd learned that phrase from TV and it finally came in handy at this particular moment.

Ivy laughed but she held her hands up in surrender. "Okay, okay. You're not scared. But you would be perfectly within your rights if you were."

Lucia blinked at her friend. "I would?"

Ivy rolled her eyes but she stepped up beside her so she could sling one free arm around Lucia's shoulders. "Of course. Love changes everything. It should be scary, quite frankly."

"It should?" Oh God, emotions were robbing her of her English skills again. But the feeling that was not fear was threatening to choke her. This was silly. It was ridiculous. They had just started dating.

And they'd gotten married.

But really, when it came down to it, they were just casually dating. What was so scary about that?

As if in answer to her question, Ivy continued, "It should be frightening because love has a tendency to turn life upside down."

She smiled down at the baby in her arms and added, "In a good way. But all change is scary, right?"

Lucia nodded. She didn't trust herself to speak.

"I mean, look at me. I thought I was headed toward a career and finding a husband was the last thing on my mind." Ivy's smile was so satisfied and so sweet. But Lucia got chills.

That was not what she wanted. She didn't want a husband and kids. Not yet. That was the whole point of running away and starting her own fashion line. Career first. She would not fall victim to the same fate that had trapped her mother.

True, it was the cancer that killed her, but Lucia's missing-in-action father had robbed her of her life before that. Or at least, that's the way it seemed. She'd fallen in love and look what had happened? All of her mother's plans for travel and adventure had been replaced by heartbreak...and a baby.

If Ivy noticed Lucia's sudden silence, she didn't let on. She continued to chatter away, happy as could be that her friend was the latest dupe to fall victim to the con called love.

Maybe that was a bit harsh. She was too young to be this bitter.

Ivy's next words brought her back to the present with a start. "I hate to break it to you, Lucia, but you are clearly a smitten kitten. I've never seen you look at anyone that way. Definitely not Marco."

A male voice from the doorway startled them both. "Did I hear my name?"

Oh no. This could not be happening. But yes, there he was, standing behind Ivy in the doorway, a politely questioning expression on his face.

"*Ciao*, Marco." Lucia tried not to shift uncomfortably under her ex-fiancé's cold gaze.

He gave her a little nod in return and graced Ivy with an actual smile.

"Oh, hi Marco," Ivy said. She started to back away from Lucia, despite Lucia's rather desperate move to clutch her arm.

Deftly avoiding Lucia's grip, Ivy took her daughter and her uncalled for opinions and waltzed out of the room with a, "Good to see you, Marco. Talk later, Luce!"

Traitor.

Lucia's smile felt frozen and she had a suspicion it didn't look terribly genuine. But really, what did he expect? They hadn't spoken since that last day, that last fight....

"How've you been?" she asked, then winced at how chipper she sounded. Yikes.

Marco ignored the question and folded his arms across his chest. "I hear congratulations are in order."

Maggie Dallen

Uh oh. Here we go.

Lucia's batted her eyelashes and feigned innocence. "Why thank you, Marco. Is that why you're here? To wish me the best in my new marriage?"

She was being petty and a little mean, but she couldn't help it. His overbearing, judgy expression was so irritating she wanted to smack it.

He held up a manila folder. "I came to get your grandfather's signature."

"Oh." That sounded right. Marco was working for his father, who was in business with Grandpa. It seemed he was forever trying to track down her grandfather to wrap up paperwork.

"I was told he was busy talking to your husband, so I figured I'd wait." His smirk was so familiar it was almost comforting. But it wasn't. It was annoying. "I mean," he added, "I don't expect this to last long."

Lucia rolled her eyes. "Their meeting or this marriage?"

He shrugged.

"Subtle. Real subtle."

Marco actually laughed at that. "I'm not being subtle? What about you? Are you seriously trying to fool anyone into thinking this marriage is for real?"

"No," Lucia bit out. "Of course not." Still. Having her ex mock her current relationship was irritating in the extreme. There should be a law against exes having an opinion.

Marco ambled toward her. "What's the deal? Is he the gold digger or are you?"

When she failed to respond, Marco tossed his head back with a laugh and pointed at her accusingly. "I knew it. You're using this poor sap, aren't you?"

"No! It's not like that." *He's using me too.* Somehow that argument didn't seem like it would help.

Instead, she opted to change the subject and say what she'd been meaning to say for the past few months. "I don't want to talk about Ryan. I'm glad you're here, I've been meaning to call or write...." Oh Lord, this was harder than she'd thought. What was it she'd told Ryan about apologizing? Oh yeah..."I'm sorry, Marco."

She watched as some of the coldness melted from his gaze. She had to swallow her pride and temporarily ignore the fact that he was mocking her—and Ryan, for that matter—but it had to be said. "I'm sorry for everything," she continued with a helpless shrug. "We've been close for so long, I don't want us to be enemies."

He studied her then in a manner she knew well. He'd never been one to speak without thinking first. Even as a kid he'd been known to pause in the middle of a conversation to carefully think through his next words. He'd never changed. Maybe she hadn't either.

"It's okay," he said, finally, shifting so he was no longer so rigid in the center of the room. His smirk turned into a self-deprecating smile. "I mean, it wasn't okay. Not at first. But...."

Lucia found herself holding her breath, waiting for him to continue.

"But I eventually realized you were right to call it off. I deserve more. We both do."

Lucia nodded. That's what it had all come down to. They could have been married—maybe they would have even been content. But they would have been settling and deep down she thought they both knew it.

"I want the best for you, you know," Lucia said. And she meant it. Things may have turned sour for them toward the end, but he would always be her high school sweetheart and she hoped one day they could even be friends. Someday. Probably not soon.

He was nodding as he reached a hand back to cup the back of his neck.

Marco never had been any good with genuine emotions. They made him itchy, he used to say.

"Me too," he said finally. "For you."

There was a silence then and Lucia mentally begged Marco to let it end with that. It was a nice apology and a make-up of sorts. Good enough for now. But she didn't want to hear any more of his opinions, particularly not about—

"So...your husband," Marco started.

Lucia's shoulders slumped. Of course he couldn't keep his opinions to himself. When had he ever where she was concerned? "I don't want to hear it, Marco."

"I'm sorry, Lucy, but I don't want to see you make a mistake." *The same mistake your mom made.* He didn't say it but he didn't have to. He knew her deepest darkest fears better than anyone.

"It's not like that." Her voice was close to a growl but she managed to resist the urge to stomp her foot. Perhaps she was growing up after all. "He's not in it for my money."

He raised a cynical brow but relented. "Fine, so he's not in it for the money. Then why is he doing this? What's he getting?"

Her. She couldn't bring herself to say it. She was not selling herself as part of this bargain. But it was the truth wasn't it? Sure he was getting money, but that wasn't why he was going along with this plan—he'd made that abundantly clear. He was here to support her, help her achieve her goals. He was there for *her*.

As if reading her mind, he gave her a little headshake of disappointment. "Don't fool yourself, Lucy. Nobody will give something for nothing. If he's not in it for money than he must care about you and you're going to break his heart."

"I am not." But Ivy's words were still echoing in her skull. What did he want from her? What did he expect?

"Does he want a real marriage?" Marco asked.

She answered him quickly. "No. Of course not."

He didn't, did he?

"What does this guy expect then?" Marco asked. "That you two will go get an annulment once the money comes through and you'll run off to pursue your dreams?"

Lucia stared at Marco. She honestly didn't know how to answer. The funny thing was, Marco didn't sound like he was trying to be mean, he just seemed curious. She supposed she would be interested too if Marco had suddenly up and married some stranger. She wished she could answer him but the sad truth of the matter was….she didn't know what Ryan expected.

What did he want? Hell, what did she want to happen once she got her money?

She shook her head, annoyed by her own wishy-washy train of thought. She knew what she wanted—of course she did. She wanted what she'd always wanted—a future, success, a career. Everything her mother had been denied thanks to her father. And cancer. But mainly her father.

Lucia squared her shoulders, feeling more confident than ever in her plan. But then Marco had to ruin it by coming over and planting a brotherly kiss on her forehead. "I truly hope you figure out what you want. For both your sakes."

* * * *

When Ryan found her a little while later, she was slumped in a chair in the library, stewing over everything Marco had said and the answers she wished she'd given. Why was it always so easy to come up with comebacks in hindsight?

Her ex had no idea what he was talking about. She got this. And she and Ryan were on the same page…finally. There was no reason to panic or second-guess their decisions. "Hey, you." He grinned down at her.

That smile. Would she ever tire of that smile? It seemed to wash away every ugly doubt Marco had stirred up and she smiled up at him before jumping up and giving his hand a tug, all but dragging him out to the villa's terrace. They stopped short once they reached the outside and the crisp fall air brought with it the scents of the valley. What was she doing wasting time worrying when she should be enjoying her time at home with her family?

Inhaling deeply, she let it out with a sigh. "I've missed it here."

Ryan came up behind her and wrapped his arms lightly around her waist in a gesture that was achingly familiar—like they were a real couple who did things like slip off to be alone at night.

And maybe they were.

A shiver ran up her spine at the thought before she pushed it back down. Exactly when had she started to lose her senses around this guy? *Day one.* But she was in control now. She wouldn't lose her focus going forward. She had other things she needed to concentrate on that took priority over a new boyfriend—especially a boyfriend who happened to be her husband. Talk about complicated.

But that didn't mean she couldn't enjoy what she had while she had it, did it? Of course not. Who knew how long this would last?

Turning in his arms, she laced her arms around his neck and twined her fingers together. "You were amazing in there with my grandfather."

To her surprise and delight, Ryan actually blushed. Or at least it looked suspiciously like a blush in the moonlight. He gave her a sheepish grin. "You heard that?"

Lucia nodded. "Enough to know you are now officially my knight in shining armor."

He laughed at that and his arms tightened around her waist drawing her in closer so the lengths of their bodies were pressed up against each other and his face was mere inches from hers. His closeness was intoxicating. The scent of him, the feel of him beneath her hands and against her skin.

He leaned in, his lips teasing hers, making a promise of more to come. Yes, please.

She let her fingers toy with the hair at the edge of his neck as her lips trailed down his jawline. His reaction was instantaneous and, quite frankly, flattering. His erection pressed against her middle as he groaned her name.

"We can't," he whispered. "Not here."

Her hands, which had moved to his chest, stilled. He was right. What was she doing, molesting this man right there where anyone could stumble across them. But then again, he was her husband. She was allowed to do whatever the hell she damn well pleased as long as they found some privacy.

Her grin was wicked as she reached down to take his hand. "Come on, there's a gazebo down the hill where no one would ever go at this time of night."

The gazebo was deserted, as she'd known it would be. The kids were in bed and the few adults who hadn't retired to their rooms were gathered around the fireplace drinking wine and catching up. The full moon lit the way and when they reached the confines of the gazebo, Lucia turned and leapt into his arms, startling a laugh out of him as he lifted her up off of her feet so her eyes were even with his.

"I could get used to this," Ryan said.

Lucia rested her forehead against his and grinned. "Used to Italian meals and nights spent making out on the Tuscan countryside? Don't get too used to it, this is no longer my home."

He peppered little kisses along her nose and cheeks. "So you don't cook amazing Italian meals like your aunts?"

Wariness shot through her like a bullet. He was teasing. She knew he was teasing. But the image of the life Marco had planned for her flashed through her mind. Barefoot and pregnant and cooking in the kitchen. She was overreacting. That's not what he was suggesting. But still.

"Of course I cook, don't be ridiculous."

He pulled her closer, held her tighter. She wanted to savor the feeling. She ached to snuggle up against his warmth and give her hands free reign over his body.

Her pulse quickened as his hands started an exploration of their own. Down her hips, over her bottom, up the sides of her waist. Desire made it impossible to think. She sighed as she let herself sink into his warmth, her arms wrapping around him as her lips found his neck.

Then he started talking again. His low voice was so sexy it made her shiver. But then the words started to filter through the haze of heat and alarm bells started to ring in the back of her brain.

"I bet you didn't know I can cook," he said. "I'll make you dinner when we get home."

Home? Since when do they have a home together? They were strangers a month ago. She tried to tune him out and moved to kiss his lips—a silent plea to stop talking, for the love of God.

But Ryan, though thorough in his kisses, seemed amped up with a different kind of energy. He pulled back from the kiss to look into her eyes.

She squirmed out of his arms, the excitement and desire quickly drowning in a sea of anxiety. Why was he talking like they had a future? Like they were...married.

Oh God.

"What do you think," he persisted. "Should I cook you a nice, romantic meal when we get home to celebrate our successful mission?"

He was teasing. She knew he was teasing. So why was panic making her heart leap into her throat like it was trying to escape? And why did he have to keep using that word? Home. As if they had a home together.

"Maybe," she hedged before leaning in to kiss him again. She really did want to kiss him. She also wanted him to shut up.

Apparently he sensed her hesitation because he gently pulled back again. "What do you mean?"

Lucia sighed, not even trying to hide her annoyance. "Ryan, we are in a garden in the moonlight and we are one signature away from being millionaires in our own right. Can't we just enjoy the moment?"

He stared at her unblinking, the blue of his eyes drowned out by the darkness of the night around them. Somehow his dark gaze made it seem like he could see right through her. She didn't want to be analyzed or figured out, dammit, she wanted to be kissed.

"Luce, what's wrong?"

Lucia resisted the urge to sigh again. "Nothing is wrong. But I didn't bring you out here to talk, Ryan."

"Well maybe I want to talk." Ryan was studying her and she hated it. She hated it even more when his arms dropped to his sides and she was left cold and alone, standing before him. Why was he ruining everything? They were having fun. Finally, for the first time in ages, she felt like she was living. Like she was alive and free. Nothing was standing in her way—not an old-fashioned fiancé, or her grandfather or a lack of money. The world was hers for the taking. She had everything she wanted.

This partnership was never supposed to be about love or emotions. That's what had gotten her mother into trouble. Following her heart is what ruined her. The plan was to convince her grandfather and if what she'd overheard was anything to go by, it was just a matter of time before he came around. Her grandfather may be a lot of things, but he was not a fool. He would not stand in the way of this once he realized that if he did he risked losing her.

Guilt churned in her stomach at that. She was using her grandfather's guilt over her mother against him. What kind of horrible person was she? She shook that off. Now was not the time. Not when Ryan was watching her like she'd just sprouted horns.

"Did something happen?" Ryan shoved his hands into his pockets.

Lucia shrugged. "Nothing happened. I just...." She struggled to find words through the jumbled, conflicting mess of thoughts racing through her brain. Even her body was in turmoil as the need to be close to him went to war with the urge to run away. "I'm not sure I'm going back to New York after this."

The words seemed to come out of her mouth of their own volition. And the moment they did she felt the tight band across her chest start to ease but her throat grew choked with emotion.

The hurt surprise that flickered across Ryan's face was a stab in her chest. What was she doing? Why couldn't she just enjoy herself and let this relationship, or whatever it was, play out? But no, she was standing here rejecting the man who'd just told her grandfather everything she had never been able to say for herself.

It wasn't a lie, necessarily. She hadn't thought beyond this trip and beyond getting the money. But the more she thought about it, the more it made sense. Talking to herself as much as to him, she continued, her voice a little too high-pitched to sound natural. "I was thinking I might meet up with Eleanor and the others at the London show. Once I have the money, I'll be able to network and continue my internship while I'm working on my own designs."

When he remained silent, she added, "I mean, it's not like I have anything waiting for me back in New York."

The words felt like glass in her throat and there was a little part of her—okay, a big part of her— that wanted him to argue. Tell her that she had him...

"I thought there was something more here. I thought—" he cut himself off abruptly with a curse. He took two steps back and the short distance felt insurmountable. There was a gaping hole between them now that had never been there before.

Reach out to him, a little voice pleaded. *Tell him you don't mean it.* But she couldn't. The part of her that wanted to run away was too strong. She couldn't let him hold her back from her future. She couldn't. She owed it to herself and to her mother.

So she stayed still, her heart aching, and tears building behind her eyes. *What was she doing?*

He ran a hand through his hair and looked down at his feet. "I'm an idiot." He muttered under his breath and she might not have heard him if the night hadn't been so still. The only sound aside from his whispered comment was her heart beating in her ears.

Lucia reached for him then, an instinct that had nothing to do with reason, but he had already turned and was heading back to the villa. Back to *his* room, because even though they were married, her grandfather had insisted they have separate rooms until he decided if their marriage was valid.

Apparently her family didn't even think she was capable of properly eloping without their approval.

She watched Ryan walking away. Her head and heart were screaming at her to run after him. Stop him. But her feet remained frozen in place. This man had hidden the truth from her. They barely knew one another. There was no way she'd let herself get swallowed up in another relationship. Not now, not when she was so close to freedom she could taste it.

What the hell was wrong with him? This was supposed to be fun. Easy. This was supposed to be all about money and sex, goddamn it. She wrapped her arms around herself as a shiver wracked her body and the hollow feeling threatened to swallow her whole.

* * * *

"You're an idiot" became Ryan's mantra for the rest of the night. What had he been thinking?

He hadn't, that was the short answer.

That little episode out on the gazebo was starting to feel like a drug-induced hallucination. Looking back on it, it was like watching a bad movie and he couldn't even recognize himself. Who was that guy? Surely not Ryan, the confident bartender who'd been raised to believe love and marriage and happily ever afters were a thing of fairy tales. He was not a romantic. Why would he be, when his family had the tendency to twist anything even resembling love into something toxic? Yet....it had happened. He'd gotten swept away like a teenage girl swooning over her first crush.

He flopped down on his bed with a groan. This was ridiculous. Lucia was offering a no-strings-attached fling. As if that wasn't enough, the woman was giving him millions of dollars on top of that. He should be overjoyed. He should be thanking his lucky stars. And instead...he'd blown it.

Even now, an hour and several glasses of wine later, he couldn't figure out what had happened. What supernatural force had taken control of his body and turned him into a needy, girly wuss? It was humiliating to remember the look on her face, that wary, trapped look. Like he'd suggested they move in together and start a family rather than just, you know...dinner.

He should go to her, explain the situation.

And say what? Sorry, I freaked you out, it's just...I've never been in love before.

Love. Jesus, is that what this was? If so, love sucked. He hadn't expected this to happen. Ever. He'd been fairly certain his family situation had acted as a sort of vaccine against this particular disease. But, if he had ever harbored even the tiniest hope of finding love for himself, he certainly wouldn't have imagined falling for someone who didn't love him back.

Wasn't love supposed to be all magic and happiness and pleasure? Maybe this was something else. It sure as hell didn't feel good.

Maybe he had a weird strain of the flu.

While he pondered that thought, there was a knock on his door. Ryan flew to his feet with an excitement that was alarming.

Lucia. She'd had a change of heart. She's come to clear the air and tell him she feels the same way. That she is wildly, crazily, stupidly in love.

He opened the door with a little too much oomph and with a wide, triumphant smile. That was quickly erased when he saw the scowling face before him.

Daniel.

"What do you want?"

Daniel's frown deepened.

Oh for the love of God....did he really expect a warm welcome after the way he'd been sending him lethal glares all day long? Besides it was nearly midnight, what the hell—

"Is everything okay? Is Lucia all right?"

Daniel pushed him aside and entered the room as if he owned the place. "She's fine....for now."

Oh no. Ryan's stomach plummeted. Something was wrong with Lucia.

"What does that mean?" Fear made his tone harsher than ever and his hands clenched into fists as he fought the urge to shake it out of him. "What is wrong with Lucia?"

Daniel turned to face him and thrust his tablet in his face. "As if you don't know."

The screen showed a gossip website that was entirely in Italian. He scanned the pictures, the headlines. He didn't have to read Italian to get the gist. His heart sank into his stomach.

"Oh bloody hell."

He was dimly aware of Daniel lecturing him as he scrolled through the site. It just got worse and worse as he went, until there at the bottom of the page was a picture of Lucia in her flimsy black dress standing next to him....in front of Elvis.

They were all grinning like drunken idiots. Even Elvis.

"How did they—"

"Find out?" Daniel finished. "You tell me."

A buzzing in his ears made it hard to hear. He tried to focus on the words before him but no amount of staring made the words make sense. "What does it say?"

Daniel was silent for so long that he finally pulled his gaze from the tablet to look at the man standing before him, fuming with anger. "It says everything," Daniel said. "The whole story of Lucia's mother, her father abandoning them." Daniel's fists clenched at his sides and the next words came out through gritted teeth. "The headline says it's the tell-all story of Italy's leading family."

Ryan froze in the face of Daniel's wrath. Daniel thought he was responsible for this. Lucia would think he had done this. All for revenge.

"I didn't...this isn't..." Ryan stopped and took a deep breath. "I didn't do this."

Daniel's smirk was mocking and entirely humorless. "Really? Because if you wanted to get to me through those I love, you've succeeded."

Ryan shook his head. "That wasn't my plan. I just wanted—"

"Revenge, I know, Holly told me. Well played. You managed to fool Holly, Jack, and Lucia into thinking you changed your ways. That you actually gave a damn about Lucia."

"I did. I mean, I do." The anxiety he'd been wallowing in for the past few hours grew to outright terror. He could lose her for good—if he'd ever had her to begin with.

He turned to the door. "I have to find Lucia. I have to explain."

Before he could open the door, Daniel reached past him and held a hand against the door to keep it shut. "That's not going to happen."

* * * *

She was an idiot. All through the restless night, that was the phrase running on repeat through her brain, even in her dreams when she would occasionally drift off. *Idiot, idiot, idiot.*

Ryan was the kindest, sweetest, not to mention hottest, man she'd ever met. More than that, he *got* her. He seemed to understand her passion for her work, her sense of humor, her need to strike out on her own...unlike anyone she'd ever met. And she'd driven him away.

Shoving aside the covers, she leapt out of bed. That was it. Enough moping. She had to talk to Ryan. Not just talk—she had to apologize. What kind of weirdo got freaked out because her husband—or lover, or boyfriend, or whatever Ran was—offered to cook her dinner?

She'd overreacted, that much was obvious. Being home, back under her grandfather's thumb, under the watchful eyes of her aunts and uncles and Daniel and Ivy....she'd instantly felt like the spoiled girl she'd always been. The bird in a gilded cage. The girl she'd been when she'd left this place months ago.

But she wasn't that girl anymore. She was an independent woman and Ryan loved her for it.

He *loved* her.

All of the air left her lungs as the enormity of that statement hit her. That was it. She had to talk to him. She threw a sweater over her pajamas while she brushed her teeth. With one hand, she twisted her long hair into a low bun.

She gave herself one quick glance in the mirror and nearly laughed aloud. Not the sexiest way to show up in her husband's doorway but there would be time for lingerie and sexy dresses later. She had to talk to him now. The idea of spending any more time away from him and letting him think she didn't care—it was unbearable.

She was halfway down the hall that led to Ryan's room when her grandfather's voice stopped her. "Lucia, I need to talk to you."

"Not now, Grandpa, I have to talk to Ryan."

There was a silence as she reached his door, which was ajar. She poked her head in and found it empty. Huh. She hadn't figured Ryan to be an early riser. He had the whole bartender-night owl vibe going on.

She retraced her steps, back to her grandfather's study where he sat behind his desk, as he did every morning, sipping his coffee and reading the newspaper. To find him here as if she'd never left. As if they'd never fought. It was oddly comforting. Like no matter what happened, he would always be here for her.

Her heart squeezed with an unexpected wave of emotion. But that was the thing. Not everything was the same. And here, now, she saw that. Her grandfather looked older than ever as he peered at her over his coffee mug, those all-seeing eyes were crinkled up in a way she knew well. He was worried about her. Like usual.

Giving in to the wave of nostalgia and love, she rushed toward him and threw her arms around his neck.

He laughed and hugged her back. "What is this for?"

She pulled back and shook her head. "I've just missed you, that's all."

He patted her cheek the way he'd always done since she was a little girl. "I missed you too, *mi principessa*."

For the first time in a long time, she didn't mind the nickname. Ryan had done that. So all he had done was listen but that simple act—listening, no, not listening, *hearing*—that had been enough to heal. She had to remember to thank him for that.

Speaking of….

"Grandpa, have you seen Ryan? I need to talk to him."

The worried frown turned to an ominous scowl. "Have a seat, Lucia."

Uh oh. Lucia didn't move. "What is it?"

"Ryan is not here."

Dread filled Lucia's senses. She'd done it. She'd driven him away. "What do you mean, he's not here? Where did he go?"

She had a dim, distant hope he would say Ryan had run out to the shop to get some milk but that hope was dashed quickly.

"He's back in the States. Daniel flew him to New York last night."

Lucia was stunned into speechlessness for several moments as a flood of questions raced through her mind. "Why?"

Her grandfather gestured for her to take a seat and she did so in a daze. How could he leave like that? Why wouldn't he give her a chance to explain?

He glanced at his laptop and then back to her. "The local tabloids have run an article about you."

Lucia blinked at him for a moment. How did that matter? For a moment she struggled to see the correlation. Then understanding dawned and she held out her hand. "Show me." It wasn't a request.

Her grandfather handed her his laptop which was already on the ghastly tabloid site. Lucia read through it quickly, her brain unable to keep up with all she was reading. It was a load of garbage, all of it. It hardly ever sounded like her life.

Abandoned by her father, orphaned with her mother's death. It made it sound like…like she'd been alone. When in reality she had known more love in her lifetime thanks to her grandfather and extended family than most people were ever lucky enough to experience. From the little she'd heard of Ryan's family, it was safe to say his family bond didn't even come close even though his mother was alive and he'd been lucky enough to know his father.

The rest of it…the stuff about her breakup with Marco, her marriage to Ryan. It all sounded so sordid and dramatic, like something out of a soap opera. It sounded….well, it sounded ridiculous.

She looked up to see her grandfather watching her with concern but, truth be told—she didn't feel all that traumatized. In fact, she found herself battling a ridiculous urge to laugh. But Grandpa looked so worried…

"Are you all right?" she asked. After all, the details about her mother's mistakes….it had to have been hard for him to read. To relive.

His brows furrowed in confusion. "Of course I'm all right, it's you I'm worried about."

She let out a breath she hadn't realized she'd been holding. "Oh, thank goodness."

They stared at one another for a moment before Lucia cracked a smile of relief. "I'm glad you're okay."

He leaned forward over the desk. "I must admit, I didn't think you'd take this so well."

Lucia sighed as she handed the laptop back. "I'm not thrilled that my life is splashed on the front page of the tabloids but it's not the first time our family is in the spotlight and I'm certain it won't be the last."

Her grandfather took the computer from her and snapped it shut. "That's true but…that's not what I was referring to."

"You mean that stuff about my mom?"

His whole body stiffened at the mention of her mother. Had it always been that way? How had she never noticed? Leaning forward, she wrapped her hand around his. "Grandpa, I may not have known my mother but I know you. You were a good father to her. She was lucky to have you."

She hurried on before he could stop her.

"And so am I." She looked down at their hands. "I know I hurt you when I left. You must have thought I was following in my mother's footsteps. But I wasn't, I promise. I wasn't trying to hurt you, I just wanted a chance to stand on my own two feet. I want to make you proud."

Her grandfather placed his other hand on top of hers and she saw tears brimming in his eyes. "Lucia, I have always been proud of you—every day you have been alive, I have been proud to call you my little girl." He stopped and raised his brows as if he'd just discovered something surprising. "But you're not a little girl any longer, are you?"

She had to smile at that. "No, Grandpa, I'm not a little girl. But I'm still your granddaughter, thank God."

He laughed and leaned back in his chair, letting go of her hands. "Even though you're not my little girl, I still want to protect you." He shook his head. "I'm sorry I couldn't protect you from this…." He waved his hand with a look of disgust. "This husband of yours."

Ryan. For a few moments there she'd actually forgotten he'd left her. The pain came back with full force. God, how had she let it get to this point? "I can't believe he left without giving me a chance to explain...to apologize."

Her grandfather's eyes crinkled in confusion. "What do you need to explain? And why on earth would you need to apologize?"

Lucia sighed. "Because I said some things last night...." She rubbed at her eyes. It was painful to even think about the way she'd pushed him away.

"What kind of things?"

She looked up then, having almost forgotten her grandfather was still there with her. "It doesn't matter. Clearly I hurt him if he left in the middle of the night."

Her grandfather steepled his fingers in front of him on the desk in a gesture she knew well. He was thinking.

"He didn't leave because of something you said," he said slowly, as though talking to a young child. Or an idiot. "He left because we made him."

"What?" Lucy shot up out of her chair. "Why? And who's we?"

"Daniel and myself." Her grandfather shrugged. "Well, mainly Daniel."

"Why?" she asked again. Her heart was pounding in her chest and her brain was a jumble of competing thoughts.

His eyes narrowed and he leaned forward. She had the feeling he was waiting for her to figure it out. But it wasn't until he made a vague gesture toward the laptop that all of the pieces clicked into place.

"You think...." she started. "You think *Ryan* leaked this story?"

Her grandfather's expression was grim. "Daniel told me Ryan had issues with him. The boy took a job under a false name just to get close to him."

Lucia stared at her grandfather. She understood the logic. In fact, she was surprised she hadn't leapt to that conclusion herself.

"He outright admitted to Jack and Holly that he intended to use his relationship with you to hurt Daniel."

"Yes, but that was before...." Lucy stopped, the rest of the words caught in her throat. How could she explain? Her grandfather's reasoning made sense. She could see how this looked to him and the others. But.... they were wrong. There was no doubt in her mind.

"Before what?"

Lucia shook her head, at a loss for words. "That was before we really knew one another and before...before he chose to put me before his family and their vendetta. That was before I knew that..."

To Lucia's surprise and horror, tears started to pool in her eyes at the overwhelming emotions that flooded through her

"Before you knew what?"

Lucia's next words came out with a wail. "Before I knew that I'm in love with my husband."

Chapter 13

The last plane ride was awkward, but this....well, this was sheer hell.

Ryan didn't want to talk and he'd assumed Daniel would give him the same silent treatment he'd been giving him since the day he'd married Lucia. Had that only been four days ago? Less than a week and it was over. He'd managed to ruin the closest thing to a real relationship he'd ever had. And he hadn't even done anything!

Except scare away the woman he loved.

He let his head fall into his hands at the memory. If only he could go back and do it all over again. If only he'd had the chance to talk to her one more time, explain everything. He needed to make this right.

But he couldn't even wallow in his regrets and "if onlys" because he'd been wrong about Daniel. Daniel apparently turned into something of a chatty Cathy in the face of Ryan's misery.

"I can understand your hatred of me," he was saying as he flipped through documents in a manila folder. He didn't even bother to look up so Ryan found himself staring at the top of Daniel's head as he multitasked. Only Daniel Gladwell could get work done while giving a lecture.

"I'm so glad you understand." Ryan didn't even bother to hide his contempt. Why bother when Daniel and, more importantly, Lucia, thought he was responsible for that horrid exposé. And why wouldn't they? His guilty conscience was still gnawing at him. He'd set this in motion by going along with his family's stupid plans. All because of their hatred for this man. A man who, at this moment at least, was easy to hate since he was the one forcibly taking him away from the woman he loved.

Well, he along with one of his security guard henchmen. They hadn't even given him the chance to explain or to even talk to Lucia. His wife! Okay fine, so in name only, but still....didn't he have a right to defend himself?

"You don't know the whole story, Ryan."

Ryan looked over at Daniel and was surprised to find him staring at him, the documents in his hand apparently forgotten as he focused on him. Shifting in his seat, Ryan sighed. "And what exactly don't I know?"

"The truth about your father."

Ryan stiffened, his eyes locked on the man across from him. He didn't want to be curious. Everything his mother had told him over the years was still fresh in his mind—how this man had discovered the company's vulnerabilities and swooped in to steal it out from under them. Out from under him. This man was merciless, conniving, and duplicitous. But he couldn't bring himself to stop Daniel when he started to speak.

"Your family's company was my first solo takeover." Daniel shrugged, "I'd worked on plenty with my partners, but this was my first chance to take the reins."

Ryan turned to look out the window, though there was nothing to see. He didn't want to hear this man's rationalizations.

"The company was in bad shape. It was bordering on bankruptcy and vultures were getting ready to swoop in."

"Vultures like you," Ryan muttered. The old anger and resentment flared up in him like a match ready to be struck at a moment's notice.

"Yes. Like me."

Ryan's head swiveled back to Daniel, who continued to watch him. "So you admit it?"

"That I'm an opportunist? Absolutely. That I was ready and willing to invest in a failing company? Of course. That's my job." His voice was level; he wasn't bragging and he didn't sound the least bit defensive.

Ryan turned back to the window but he continued to listen, his body on edge as he waited for Daniel to make his point.

"The difference between me and the other vultures," Daniel continued, "was that I wanted to help your father—help your family."

Ryan's laugh was humorless and short. "I'm sure."

Daniel was silent for so long Ryan finally turned back to him, only to find Daniel's gaze fixed on him. "I'm serious. I wanted to help your father because he....well, he was fighting some demons of his own."

The gambling. The drinking. The vices his family refused to speak of after his death.

Ryan's jaw clenched but he kept silent.

"I offered to help him," Daniel said.

The air rushed from Ryan's lungs. "What? What do you mean?"

"I mean, unlike the other vultures, I offered to give your father a second chance at running the company."

Ryan blinked at Daniel across the few feet that separated them. "And?"

Daniel shrugged. "And he turned me down. Told me to go to hell."

Ryan shifted uncomfortably in his seat. "That company, his employees....they were everything to him."

Daniel's gaze was so close to pitying, it took everything in Ryan to meet his eyes.

"I promised him I would keep the employees. And I did. Every last one. But your father, he opted to leave. He said he had too much pride to stay and be someone else's lapdog."

Ryan could hear his father's voice even as Daniel spoke. That bitterness, the stubborn pride—it was the same voice he heard coming from his brother's mouth now and the same mantra he'd heard from his mother since forever.

"What are you saying?" Ryan asked, the age-old anger flickering in the face of Daniel's cold reason. "Are you saying you're some kind of savior here?"

Daniel shook his head. "No, definitely not a savior. I was and am a businessman." He cracked a small smile. "No one would ever call me a saint. I guess I just wanted to let you know that I'm not the devil either."

Ryan was silent as he studied his family's arch nemesis. Funny how one's nemesis could be so logical and....human when you were sitting across from him face to face. Much as he hated to admit it to himself, Daniel's words rang true. It fit his father's personality and was in keeping with the memories he had from that era....the drinking, the gambling, the fights about how he was going to lose the company.

He had lost the company. And blaming the man who'd saved it.... who'd saved the employees...that hadn't done anyone any good. All the blame, all the resentment....where had it gotten them? It had killed his father and destroyed his mother and brother. Turned them into bitter shells of themselves, so focused on avenging the past that they'd never faced the future.

And Ryan. Where had it left him? Sitting alone in a plane with Daniel Gladwell as he left the only woman he'd ever loved. She'd have woken by now and he was certain her grandfather had shown her the site. She must hate him.

"Why are you telling me this? Why now?"

"Because you don't seem like an irrational man, Ryan." Daniel's voice was even but somehow Ryan sensed it was a high compliment coming from this man.

"Thanks?"

Daniel ignored the sarcasm. "Normally I wouldn't explain myself or my actions…to anyone. But I will not see my friends hurt over some misplaced sense of vengeance."

The mention of Lucia and *the incident*, as he was starting to think of it, had him gripping the armrests. How many more ways could he say it? "I. Didn't. Do. It."

Daniel barely flinched in the face of Ryan's clipped, angry tone. "Then who did?"

Ryan threw his hands up in the air. "How should I know? All I know is, it wasn't me. I would never hurt Lucia like that. I—I love her."

A heavy weight lifted from his chest. There. He'd said it. He'd finally said the words out loud…and to his family's enemy.

He fell back in his seat with a sigh. How romantic.

Daniel sat in silence for so long, Ryan thought he might have fallen asleep with his eyes open. But then, finally, Daniel said, "So what are you going to do about it?"

* * * *

Lucia was crying but her grandfather was…smiling? What was wrong with this scenario?

"Whydoyoulooksohappy?"shedemanded. "I'mheartbrokenoverhere."

"Why, because you're in love with your husband?" her grandfather said with a laugh. "I can think of worse fates."

Lucia let out a miserable little moan and reached for the ever-present box of tissues on her grandfather's desk. "This isn't the way it was supposed to happen. I don't *want* to be in love."

"Why not?" Her grandfather was leaning forward over the desk, still wearing that annoying smile.

Lucia shredded the tissue in her hands as she struggled to find words. "Because I don't want another boyfriend telling me what's best for me—"

Grandpa frowned. "Does Ryan do that?"

Lucia stared at him. "No, but—"

Her grandfather's sigh was so loud it stopped her in her tracks. "I know I've been an overprotective grandfather and Lord knows that idiot Marco is as old-fashioned as they come—"

"I thought you *liked* Marco."

Her grandfather raised a brow at her in disbelief. "Marco is a good kid and I put up with him because he seemed to make you happy, but I was never a fan of that relationship."

They stared at one another in silence for a moment before they both started to laugh.

"Look, *mi princip*—" Her grandfather cut himself off. "Ryan was right about one thing. I won't apologize for being overprotective—that's my right as your grandfather—but he's right that you are an adult now and it's time I trust you."

"What are you saying?" Lucia sniffled a bit and blew her nose.

"I'm saying you are not your mother, God bless her soul. She made her fair share of mistakes but she was young and innocent, neither of which are crimes. I can't say I regret offering your father the money to leave—if he's the sort of man who would walk away from his family over some money than he wasn't worth having around."

Lucia watched in silence as her grandfather struggled to rein in his emotions. "But you are not your mother. She was a terrible judge of character and weak in a way that you are not." He shrugged helplessly. "I'd like to think she would have grown out of it. That she would have come back from the hurt and rejection and been stronger for it. But sadly, she wasn't given the chance."

Her grandfather looked at her then. "You don't need me to step in and protect you. You have always been strong and you've always been able to see people clearly, even as a young girl."

Lucia might have agreed with him up until these past few weeks when she had been blindsided by Ryan's ulterior motives. And then, against all odds, falling for the man who was just supposed to be her accomplice. Okay, and maybe her fling. But he wasn't supposed to be *the one*.

Lucia's heart twisted again at the way she'd all but rejected him the night before and the tears that she'd managed to stop started flowing once again. "I ruined everything. And now he's going to think that I believe this nonsense about him exposing my life story to the tabloids—"

Her grandfather crossed his arms. "Are you so sure it wasn't him?"

Annoyance flared up in a heartbeat. She leveled her grandfather with a glare. "Remember what you said about trusting my judgment? I need you to trust me now, about this."

Her grandfather held up his hands in mock surrender. "There is the girl I raised. Trust your own judgment, that's what I've always told you."

Lucia rolled her eyes. It was just like him to take credit.

"And if you're serious about this boy," he continued. "Your marriage has my approval."

Lucia sat back in stunned silence. *Just like that?* After all these years of his overprotective, overbearing ways, it was hard to believe he was willing to accept her marriage to a man he barely knew. His trust in her judgment warmed her heart as the enormity of his statement settled in.

With his approval, she had access to her trust fund. But her shocked silence wasn't just because he'd said the words that would make her a millionaire in her own right but because....she'd forgotten all about the money. "You are?"

Her grandfather nodded. "It's a silly addendum, this whole, you needing my approval rule."

"Aren't you the one who added the 'silly addendum'?"

Her grandfather looked surprised. "No, of course not. That was your mother's idea."

Her mother? She fell back in her seat, stunned into momentary silence for a second time. "But...why?"

He tilted his head to the side as he thought of how best to answer. "I think she wanted to be sure that you would be comfortable, especially once you were ready to start a family. But she was worried you would make the same mistake that she did and fall for the wrong man."

Lucia nodded slowly. It made sense, she supposed. Funny, she'd never thought about her mother in that way—as an actual mother who worried about her daughter's future and her happiness. Since she'd died when Lucia was so young, she'd never given it much thought. A bittersweet ache filled her chest at the realization that her mother, despite her mistakes, had tried her best to protect her. But she hadn't needed it. Despite her fears, she hadn't repeated her mother's mistakes—at least, not with Ryan. "I didn't fall for the wrong man. I just....went about it all wrong."

To her surprise, her grandfather shrugged. *Shrugged.* As if marrying a near stranger while in disguise and then falling for her husband was no big whoop.

"The course of true love never did run smooth," her grandfather quoted with a regal air.

"Somehow I don't think Shakespeare was envisioning an elopement in Vegas when he wrote that."

He brushed aside her comment with a wave of his hands and settled back into his chair with a determined look she knew well. "So then, you love this man. What are you going to do about it?"

Chapter 14

Ryan had traveled to Italy and back and then on to Vegas in the course of seventy-two hours. Exhausted didn't even begin to cover it. He was desperately in need of a shower, his eyelids felt like sandpaper and he hadn't had a real meal since Daniel had forced him to down a bite at his hotel, where he picked up his paycheck, the entirety of which was spent on a plane ticket to Vegas.

All of which was to say—he was not in the mood for his family.

He particularly did not want to hear their congratulations in what they assumed was his vengeance plan. "So you got the Brunelli's money?" his mother asked when he answered the phone. Before he could answer she said, "Sure it's not as good as taking money from the man himself but we'll make do, won't we Billy?"

Ryan was on speakerphone and he could dimly hear his brother's grunt of approval on the other end. The taxi stopped in front of the Vegas hotel where he'd spent his honeymoon with Lucia. It only seemed right that this marriage begin and end at the same location.

"How did you get that info on the Brunellis?" Billy asked, a touch of admiration in his voice. He'd gotten their texts the moment he'd gotten off the plane. They knew all about the tabloid scandal. Lord knew how they found out or how they'd even managed to read the Italian story, but he supposed he shouldn't have been surprised. When it came to getting revenge, his family was unstoppable. If only they'd applied that work ethic to something useful.

Billy kept talking, undeterred by Ryan's silence. "I mean, it would have been better if you'd gone after Gladwell's wife, but his business partner....not bad. That article about Brunelli's granddaughter was brutal. Daniel must be furious."

Ryan froze mid-step. His brother's nasty laugh was the last straw. It wasn't until the valet started to approach him with a look of concern that he resumed walking, his hands in fists at his sides. "I had nothing to do with that story, I already told you—"

"But you married the girl," his mother interjected, pride clear in her voice. "I've heard Daniel treats that family like they're his own. Good work, son."

Their satisfaction in the face of Lucia's humiliation made his stomach turn. His disgust—with himself and with his family—was almost more than he could take. Stopping short inside the overly air-conditioned lobby, he spoke in a low voice so only they could hear. "I will say this once, and only once. I did not set out to hurt Lucia and I will physically destroy anyone who does. Is that clear?"

The dead silence on the other end was answer enough.

"I'm not accepting any of the money from Lucia's trust fund. Not for myself and not on your behalf." His announcement caused an eruption of noise on the other end.

Ryan had worked it all out with Daniel on the flight. Daniel would loan Lucia the money she needed to start up her fashion line, and once she had access to her trust fund she could pay him back. It may not be Lucia's ideal method of getting that money but Ryan knew it was for the best. There could never be honesty between them when their relationship was founded on lies and greed and revenge.

What relationship? She wanted nothing to do with him. Ryan silenced the doubts. He would win her back eventually. He had to.

He waited until his family's protests died down before he continued, "Dad lost the company. End of story. He could have continued on there, tried to help its comeback. He could have stayed with the company but he didn't. He led the business into bankruptcy and he didn't have the strength to stay once it had fallen."

It was painful to say the words aloud but it needed to be said. Someone had to start speaking the truth if this family was ever going to let go of the past. The silence at the other end only confirmed what he'd said. He'd known, even as Daniel had been talking, that his version of events made more sense. He'd been a kid at the time but old enough to be aware of what was going on around him.

The drinking, the gambling, the pills….he'd seen it all. It was just easier to go along with his mother's story. The version that let his dead father off the hook and placed all the blame on a cold, distant stranger.

The cold, distant stranger who'd just helped him figure out what steps he needed to take next in order to win back his wife.

All the anger left him and he was left deflated, listening to a shocked and hurt silence. "I can't do it anymore. If you two want to keep holding a vendetta, there's nothing I can do about it. But I want no part of it. I want to move on with my life and I suggest you do the same."

He didn't wait for a response. He clicked the off button and took a deep breath of stale, casino air. He let himself fall back against a pillar. Maybe it was the fumes coming from the bar but he actually felt better already.

And then he heard a voice from the other side of the column. "You sounded pretty great back there."

His whole body stiffened with excitement at the familiar Italian accent. It sounded like....but it couldn't be...

Turning toward the voice, he saw a petite and sexy-as-hell Italian woman come around the other side. It was *his* petite and sexy-as-hell Italian. His pulse raced and his brain went blank at the sight of her.

"Lucia, what are you doing here?"

Her smile was unusually shy as she shifted from one foot to the other with her hands clasped behind her back. Unlike the last time they were here, she was dressed casually in jeans and an oversized sweater and her long hair was pulled back from her fresh-scrubbed face in a long braid that fell down her back.

The casino sounds around them seemed surreal—deafeningly close yet far away. He waited for her to speak. Hope threatened to drown him but a sensible part of his brain told him not to get carried away. She was probably here to give him hell for that story.

For the life of him, he couldn't figure out what he was supposed to say. When she didn't say anything, he repeated, "What are you doing here?"

What he wanted to ask was "what does it mean?" and "are you here to stay?" But he held his tongue.

In lieu of an answer she pulled one hand out from behind her and dangled a room key from her fingers. "I got us a room."

He wouldn't jump to conclusions, he promised himself. "Uh, you got us a room?"

Lucia nodded, spinning on her heel and leading the way toward the elevator bank. "I thought the two of us should talk, don't you agree?"

He couldn't see her expression and her tone was unreadable, making it impossible to figure out if she was here to work things out or to plan their divorce. Either way, she was right. They needed to talk. "Yes. Yeah, sure. Of course."

Ryan was basically speechless the entire way up to their room. Oh sure, he made some feeble attempts at striking up a conversation—"how was your flight?" and "what are you doing here?" The latter of which he realized he'd asked all of four times, at which point he forced himself to shut his mouth and keep it closed.

Lucia, meanwhile, was either doing her best mime impression or was not speaking to him. Not that he could blame her since she must think he had used her deepest darkest family secrets to get revenge for his own messed up family. But that didn't explain why she was here. Or why she was acting so weird.

Still, he promised himself he wouldn't speak until she did.

That didn't last long. She keyed into the room and stepped aside to let him in. Her bags, he noticed, were already there, along with her purse, makeup case and wallet, all of which had been tossed atop the dresser.... like she'd been in a hurry.

"Luce, I don't know why you're here but I have to tell you, I swear I didn't—"

Before he could finish, she leapt into his arms and kissed him. Shock was quickly overcome by desire and he couldn't care less why she was in his arms, just that she was in his arms. He pressed her closer, holding her tight and lifting her so her feet were off the ground and their bodies were pressed together.

This. This was home.

That realization was like the sun coming out from behind the clouds. She was his home. His family. And he would do whatever it took to make things right, to make her understand.

Her lips were enthusiastically moving over his and he tried to keep up. He was so hungry for her, he didn't think he would ever get enough. It wasn't until she pulled back slightly to come up for air that he could even begin to formulate a thought. "What. The. What..."

So it wasn't a sentence. But it was a start. He was certain that given enough time, and perhaps some distance from her amazing body which was still pressed tight against him, he might even form a coherent thought.

Despite his babbling, she seemed to realize the need for speech because she pushed against his shoulders lightly, just enough so she could slither down the length of him....which did nothing to help his fight for brainpower.

When her toes touched the ground, he reluctantly released his arms from around her and she took one step back and then another. He saw her glance up at the ceiling while inhaling a slow, deep breath.

She was trying to regain control. Good to know he wasn't the only one.

When she looked back at him, he saw that her eyes were still dark with desire but her breathing was even and she edged ever so slightly toward the end of the bed, even further out of reach.

"What are you doing here?"

Okay, so it was the fifth time he'd asked that question but at least he'd managed to string some words together. And besides, he really wanted to know.

Lucia licked her lips in a nervous gesture that was way too seductive, Ryan decided.

"Daniel told me you'd be here."

Ryan blinked. That did not compute. "What? Why? How?"

He thought he saw her lips twitch in a smile but the she looked down at the ground. "I asked him. I....uh....I needed to talk to you."

Everything that had happened back in Italy flooded back to him. He needed her to know the truth. "Luce, I promise it wasn't me."

She looked up at him and he hurried on. "I swear it. I never told anyone the things you told me. About your mother and your—"

"I know." Her soft voice cut him off and he stopped mid-sentence with his mouth agape.

"You do?"

She nodded and took a step closer. "That's not why I'm here."

"Oh." She took another step closer and much as he wanted to reach out to her, he had to understand. "How do you know? I mean, I assumed you would blame me. Everyone else did."

"I trust you." And there it was. Simple as that. A piece of his heart that had hardened through years of dealing with his family's bitterness, melted then and there. Her gaze held such heartwarming faith, he nearly crumbled in the face of it. It was humbling.

"But I'm the only one—"

Lucia cut him off with a kiss. "Don't worry, no one believes you leaked my secrets. Daniel and Grandpa are looking into it to get the truth." She pulled back long enough to look him straight in the eyes. "I love you."

The air rushed out of his lungs as her words struck his heart. He reached out to her and drew her up against him. There were no words to describe the aching joy of hearing those words. So he kissed her, long and deep until they were both panting for air and clinging to one another like they might drown.

He pulled back just long enough to say "I love you too." Her answering smile was so beautiful, he had to kiss her again. And again.

* * * *

She'd done it. She'd said the words out loud and rather than being a terrifying experience, it was freeing. Happiness rose up in her chest until she thought she might explode with it as she reveled in his kisses and the feel of his arms around her.

He'd said it too. She grinned even as he kissed her which had him leaning back with a smile of his own. "What's so funny?"

She shook her head, at a loss for words. "I'm just happy."

He cocked an eyebrow and she struggled to find the right words. It seemed anger wasn't the only thing to make English fly out the window. Passionate kisses and an overabundance of joy had the same effect.

"I didn't think it would feel this way," she said.

"Love?"

She nodded. "I thought it meant you were powerless and out of control...and you *are* but... in a good way. It's liberating."

That earned her a kiss on the nose, followed by a trail of kisses along her neck which were interspersed with whispered words of love, each of which added to her happiness until she was dizzy with joy. She would never tire of hearing those words from this man.

"So what now?" he asked. His voice was husky and so sexy it hurt. She knew what he meant. What was to become of their marriage? What would happen to them? Where would she live? What would they do for a living? So many unanswered questions.

And Lucia didn't want to think about any of them. Snaking her arms around his neck, she rose up on tiptoe so she could whisper in his ear. "Now we enjoy our honeymoon which was so rudely interrupted."

That was all she had to say before he scooped her up into his arms and strode toward the bed. Restless anticipation had her panting for air before he even set her on the bed. Their hands fumbled with buttons and zippers and a frustrating amount of layers before they were lying side by side on the bed.

He paused with his hands tangled in her hair, his lips so close to hers she could feel his breath. They were nearly naked, only a few flimsy pieces of underwear between them. "Are you sure? If you want to take things slow—"

Lucia gave his lower lip a little nip. "That's sweet, but I know what I want." She moved against him, throwing one thigh over his hips so she could press her aching heat up against his erection. "I want this."

His eyes darkened as he let out a low growl of pleasure that had her trembling for his touch. One hand moved to grab her backside, holding her against him as he worshiped her breasts with his tongue. The feel of his five o'clock shadow against her sensitive skin had her shivering with pleasure.

His tongue teased her nipple until she was panting, her hands in his hair as she held him to her. She wanted more...needed more. "I can't wait," she whispered.

His answer was a moan as he dragged his mouth back to hers to kiss her long and hard as they slipped off the remainder of their clothes. She didn't wait for him to move over her but instead pushed him back so he was lying flat on his back.

She straddled him, his desire-glazed eyes adding even more heat. Under his gaze, she was sexy. She was a woman. She was free.

His hands cupped her waist and palmed her breasts as she moved into place atop him. When she lowered herself onto him, taking him deep inside of her she thought she might lose herself completely in the mind-blowing, exquisite torture. She moved slowly against him at first until he groaned her name and it was clear he was as lost as she was. Then she picked up the pace, grinding herself against him faster and harder until they both came with a blinding ecstasy.

* * * *

She should move. There were things they needed to discuss, real life to be dealt with. But instead she nestled closer against Ryan's side and sighed in contentment as his fingers lazily traced a pattern on her back and his lips dropped the occasional kiss on the top of her head.

Her lips were buried against his throat, her head tucked into his shoulder. There would be plenty of time for talking tomorrow. Or the next day. Or whenever this honeymoon had to come to an end.

The very next day they had to check out and not without a good deal of grumbling on Lucia's part. The decision came over breakfast in bed. A breakfast which they'd thoroughly earned thanks to a night filled with more sex than snooze.

"So what are you doing in Vegas?" Lucia asked as Ryan popped a strawberry into her mouth. "Daniel didn't tell me why you came, just that you were here."

He answered while she chewed. "I came to file for an annulment."

She froze mid-chew. She'd assumed that's why he was here, of course, but to hear him say it aloud was oddly surprising. "Because you don't want to be married to me?"

He flopped back against the pillows. "That's not it and you know it. I just…I wanted to prove I'm not in this for any other reason than that I want to support you."

Lucia tilted her head to the side with a smile. "So you plan to do that by taking away my only means of getting a show of my own?"

He leaned forward then and grabbed her hand so she was forced to meet his gaze. "You don't need my help for that. You don't need help from anyone, that's my point."

She nodded. It was something she'd been thinking about ever since her chat with her grandfather.

"And I definitely don't need, or want, the money. Not when it means it would create a sense of distrust between us. There would always be uncertainty between us about my motives."

Those piercing blue eyes hadn't left hers and a nervous flutter filled her stomach. He was right, she knew he was right. But that didn't stop her heart from aching at the thought of killing this marriage before it ever got off the ground.

She nibbled on a croissant and told herself she was being ridiculous. This marriage never had anything to do with love. *Maybe not at first.* The treacherous voice sounded remarkably like her grandfather's and it was currently pleading with her to give their marriage a shot. After all, they had love and trust, the foundation for a strong marriage….

Lucia froze with the croissant halfway to her lips. Huh. Maybe she was a romantic after all.

She lunged for the coffee carafe. Clearly that was her sleep-addled brain talking. He was right. If they wanted to make a real go of things, they would need to start fresh…get to know each other.

They ate the remainder of their breakfast, packed their bags and headed down to the lobby, on their way to the county clerk's office where they would get the information they needed to call it quits.

But then Lucia spotted it. Down the end of a long hallway, she recognized the door and the telltale trail of glitter leading to it. Refusing to overthink her actions, Lucia grabbed Ryan by the hand and dragged him along behind her as she led the way.

"Where are we going?" The words were barely out of his mouth when she threw open the door and he let out a loud laugh.

She had to admit, in the cold, sober light of day, their wedding chapel looked tackier….and dirtier…than ever. "I just wanted to see it again."

He came up behind her and slipped his arms around her waist. "And? Does it live up to your memories?"

She had to laugh at that. "Not quite. Was it always so.... what's the word...?"

"Garish?" he offered. "Gaudy? Ridiculous?"

"Colorful?"

She felt him nuzzle her hair and could feel his lips against her ear. "I don't know, I was too busy watching you."

Lucia spun around then so she could wrap her arms around him. "Good answer."

He gave her that sexy-as-hell smile—the one that had nearly melted her on her barstool when she'd first met him. There was a connection here, between them. Something more than physical and something that had been there from the first moment they'd met and had grown exponentially with every passing hour.

She couldn't let that go.

"I don't want to do this." It came out as a whisper and Ryan leaned in a little closer.

"You don't want to do what?"

Lucia pursed her lips, suddenly shy and nervous now that the words were about to leave her mouth. "I don't want to annul the marriage."

Ryan's eyes widened but he didn't protest in horror. That was a good sign.

"And not because of the money. I know this sounds crazy but..."

"I don't want to either."

Lucia wasn't sure who was more surprised by his words because he had a dazed expression in his eyes like he was having an out of body experience. But when she raised her eyebrows in a silent question he nodded with far more certainty.

"Not yet, at least."

Lucia leapt at that. "Yes, exactly! Maybe we will, someday. But I don't see why we have to end it all today."

"Right," he added. "We still have the option to but we'll just....press pause. For a bit. I love you, Luce, and I love being married to you. Is that crazy?"

"Probably," she said with a laugh. "But I feel the same exact way. I love you and want to be your wife."

He looked slightly uncertain but excited, nonetheless. Pretty much exactly how she was feeling. Giddy and terrified and ecstatic.

"So we're agreed," she said.

"Agreed."

Lucia thought she might float out of that glitterbomb of a room she was so happy but she settled for linking her arm in his and smiling up at him. "Then let's go home."

Chapter 15

Ryan didn't want to see their marriage end any more than Lucia did but now, they were back in the real world and he had no idea how this marriage thing was supposed to work. He loved calling her his wife. Whether it was crazy or not, he stood by the decision. They'd made the right choice. That was what he told himself as he scrubbed at the bar with a wet rag. They'd put the annulment plan on hold. But what now?

He wasn't naïve enough to think they could leap right into a full-fledged marriage without getting to know one another. That was just idiotic.

This was something they should have talked about in Vegas—or on the plane ride home at the very least. But they'd been so busy celebrating their newfound relationship they'd spent more time making out than in talking. When they had talked it had been about their individual futures. Lucia needed space to figure out her next steps with her design career and he'd decided to go back to his job at the bar, since Daniel agreed to keep him on. It wasn't his long-term plan, obviously, but he needed time to sort out what direction he wanted to head in next. Without the weight of his family on his shoulders, he was free to pursue any career he wanted.

The only thing they'd established is they both needed time. But how much time? A full twenty-four hours had passed since they'd returned to New York City with no word from her.

She was probably knee-deep in planning her fashion line and maybe she'd already lined up her ticket to London to meet with Eleanor.

He slammed the rag into the sink with more force than necessary. It wasn't that he thought she was using him for the money. He knew her better than that. But the fashion line was her priority and he wasn't about to stand in her way. So he was left to wait. Which was fine, he told himself. He had a resume to work on and a career of his own to pursue.

Still. That little internal pep talk did little to ease the uncomfortable tightness in his chest. What happened next?

"You're late," he called out to Javier when he heard the back door click open. "Don't try sneaking in, you know I always catch you."

When Javier didn't come back with one of his typical crude comebacks, Ryan turned to the door and froze. "Lucia."

She was hovering in the doorway looking incredibly adorable in her oversized winter coat and hat. She also looked more than a little shy.

"I didn't mean to sneak in," she said. "And I don't think I'm late." She looked down at her watch. "Actually, I'm pretty sure I'm early."

"What are you–? I mean...hi." Ryan shook his head at his own stupidity. One day away from her and he was back to being a pre-pubescent teen with a crazy crush. But holy hell, she looked amazing.

He moved from behind the bar so he could go to her. He couldn't have stopped himself from going to her side if he tried. She returned his hug but when he went to kiss her she put a hand on his chest to stop him and pulled away a bit. "I'm not sure that's a good idea."

"Oh." Ice water ran through his veins and he shoved his hands into his pocket. "Yeah, sure."

What the hell? What had happened between the glitter room and now? Maybe she'd changed her mind and decided marriage was too big of a step. Maybe she'd spent the past twenty-four hours realizing she wasn't ready for that commitment. Ryan could feel his heart drop into the pit of his stomach. He'd known it deep down, that was why he'd been so terrified all morning. This was too good to be true.

He ran a hand through his hair. Right. Don't panic. He'd convince her that they could still be together, they'd just take it slowly for a while...

"I mean," Lucia continued as she took off her jacket to reveal a starched white waiter's shirt underneath. "I don't think it would be very professional of us to make out in front of the other staff, right?"

Ryan's jaw dropped. She was wearing a teasing grin that had him laughing out loud as he pulled her into his arms and planted a kiss on her lips. "So you're working here....with me?"

"If you'll have me," Lucia said.

Ryan thought his lungs might combust he was so happy and so freaking relieved. "Well, I'll have to warn the busboys that there will be a lot more broken glasses to clean up—ow." He rubbed the spot on his arms where she'd punched him. "But yeah, I think we can find you some shifts."

"Good." She grinned up at him and for a moment, he forgot everything else, even the fact that up until a minute ago he'd been convinced she was on a plane to London.

But then the questions started and his brain was racing to make sense of this sudden twist. "What about your fashion line? The designs? What about the money?"

Lucia sighed as she ran her hands over his chest in a way that was far too tempting for the workplace. "Listen carefully because I won't say this often," she teased. "But you were right."

Ryan slapped a hand over his heart and gasped so loudly a barback at the far end of the restaurant looked over to see what had happened. He would embarrass himself any day of the week to hear Lucia's laugh.

"I'm serious," she said. "I was thinking about what you said. About how if I want to make it on my own, I really need to make it on my own."

"So the money is still in the trust?"

Lucia shook her head. "It's mine but I've put it in savings so I can choose when I'm ready to have access to it. But, in the meantime, I need to learn my craft and study with the best."

"That's a pretty brave decision," Ryan said. "I'm proud of you."

Lucia stuck out her tongue. "You're also stuck with me." She glanced around the still-empty restaurant. "Where should I get started?"

She was already turning to head to the wait station but he put a hand on her arm to stop her. There was no way he could make it through an entire shift without some answers. "I've got to ask. What does this mean for us?"

He was certain she knew what he meant. What now? How were they supposed to be a married couple when they barely knew each other? Were they dating or more serious? How did they make sure whatever they had didn't interfere with her career dreams? There were so many questions they needed to address and they hung between them now.

She turned back to him and that shyness he'd seen when she'd hovered in the door was back. She looked up at him from beneath her thick black lashes. "I have no idea."

She looked so vulnerable, he had to clench his hands into fists to keep from reaching out to her and pulling her back into his arms. "Maybe we should take it slow," he said.

The moment the words left his mouth, Ryan cursed himself and Lucia's eyes widened in surprise and an amused smile tugged at her lips. "We're married, Ryan. And we've had our honeymoon. Isn't it a little late to take things slow?"

Ryan sighed. Much as he kind of hated the idea, he also thought it was for the best to slow things down and give them time to get to know one another as individuals before they truly became a couple.

Maybe he was old-fashioned after all.

"You deserve to be wooed." The moment the words left his mouth he knew they were right. He wouldn't have guessed he had an old-fashioned streak in him, but there you had it. He wanted this woman to have everything she deserved and that meant a good, healthy, normal relationship. Well, as normal as their relationship could be, given the circumstances.

She broke into a full-blown smile. "So you're going to woo me now?"

Ryan crossed his arms in front of his chest. "Damn straight. Miss Lucia Antoinette Brunelli….will you go on a date with me?"

Lucia laughed and leaned up on her tiptoes so she could grab his face and kiss his lips. "I would love to."

Fighting the urge to grab his wife and pull her into his arms, he forced a serious look. "There's one more thing we need to discuss, Lucia."

Her brows shot up but she waited patiently.

"I would like to cook dinner for you. Now I know this is a big commitment, but—"

She cut him off with another kiss—one that lasted so long he nearly forgot what they were talking about.

Epilogue

Lucia quickly discovered that Ryan's idea of taking it slow was torture. A rare and unusual form of torture, at that. But tonight that torture would come to an end.

She sat cross-legged in the makeshift candlelit dining room, which also doubled as Ryan's studio apartment. He came back from the kitchen wearing that unbearably sexy grin and carrying two plates filled with decadent desserts.

One thing she'd learned over these past two weeks....her husband was quite the romantic. And, even more surprising, so was she.

He picked up the conversation where it had left off when he'd run into the kitchen for dessert. "What did Daniel want?"

He'd summoned her from the restaurant earlier that night and into his office. The rest of the employees probably thought she'd been called in there to be fired. Although, to be fair, her waitressing skills had improved. A little. She was working on it.

She'd never found a moment alone with Ryan during the rest of his shift to fill him in on the real reason Daniel had summoned her. "Danny did some digging and he found out who leaked the story."

Ryan's eyebrows shot up. "Who was it?"

"The private detective guy Marco hired to follow me." She stabbed her piece of cake with a little more force than necessary. "Apparently the greedy jerk decided the money Marco gave him wasn't enough. Once he figured out who my family is he realized he could be making far more money so he did some digging on his own."

The rage in Ryan's eyes was sweet. She may have despised Marco's chauvinism but Ryan's chivalry was an entirely different matter. He made her feel protected but free. Cherished but strong. He made her feel like the woman she wanted to be.

Although lately....he'd mainly just made her feel frustrated.

"When I get my hands on that guy," Ryan started.

Lucia cut him off with a shake of her head. "Let it go. Please. Daniel is already handling it and you and I....we have other matters to handle."

Ryan's blue eyes met her over the candles and empty wine glasses. Toying with the dessert he'd set before her on the coffee table, she looked up at him through her eyelashes. "Do you know what today is?"

He stole a bite of her slice of cake and pretended to think it over. "Tuesday?"

Lucia rolled her eyes at the teasing. He knew very well what day it was, he was just trying to delay the torture. He was enjoying this little game of his.

When Ryan had suggested they take it slow, she hadn't realized just how slow he'd meant.

Swiping a finger into the whipped cream atop her slice, she brought it to her lips and slowly lapped it up with her tongue. A sense of triumph swept through her as she watched his eyes darken with desire as they followed her every move.

Slipping onto her hands and knees she slowly crawled toward him. "It is Tuesday," she agreed, coming to a stop inches from where he sat, apparently immobilized by lust.

"It's also our third date," she whispered.

That broke the spell. Ryan reached for her and pulled her into his lap. "Oh thank God," he said between frantic kisses. She laughed as he added, "Let's never take things slow again. Slow is terrible. Slow is dumb."

She wrapped her arms around his neck and held on tight. "I couldn't agree more."

His lips met hers and she lost herself in his touch. This was home. Ryan was family. Gasping as his lips trailed across her jaw and down her neck, she pulled back long enough to meet his gaze, which made her tremble with heady desire.

Reaching out, she pressed a palm to his lightly stubbled cheek. "I love you so much."

He leaned forward so his forehead touched hers. "Glad to hear it, my lovely wife, because I have a proposal for you."

Her laugh was shaky, her body still trembling with need. "Another proposal?"

"Mmm." He sneaked in a quick kiss before pulling back to look into her eyes. "You are my family now," he said, his words echoing her thoughts from a moment before.

She nodded eagerly. "I feel the same."

The tender look in his eyes was nearly her undoing but she forced herself to concentrate on his words. "What is this proposal you have in mind?"

His arms tightened around her waist. "I want to marry you."

She opened her mouth to remind him that they were, in fact, already married, but his next word stopped her.

"Again."

She blinked up at him. "Why?"

His grin was slow and torturously sexy. "Because you are everything that is good in my life and I want to share that with the world."

She blinked away tears of happiness. That was far and away the sweetest thing she'd ever heard. But he wasn't done.

"Plus, I want my wife to have the wedding of her dreams, surrounded by her friends and family." He paused for a moment, the question in his eyes. "I'm thinking the villa...maybe this summer?"

Visions of her perfect wedding danced through her mind. Her grandfather giving her away, her friends and family surrounding them with their love and support. "That would be perfect," she whispered.

"In that case...." Ryan gently set her off his lap so he could kneel in front of her. "Will you marry me? Again?"

Lucia laughed, tears in her eyes. "Always."

Be sure not to miss Christa Maurice's steamy Drawn To the Rhythm Book series!

Not Second Best

No more solos for this heart . . .

As a lawyer at Touchstone management, Tessa's position brings her up close and personal to some of the world's biggest heartthrobs. Sometimes that intimacy crosses professional lines, which is understandable considering Tessa's impressive contact list. But when rock star Brian Ellis set her aside for the girl of his dreams, Tessa can't help wonder if "spinster aunt" is her true vocation. Which explains her hook-up with rising star Brett Cherney at Brian's celebrity wedding . . .

As the lead singer of BroRide, Brett has lived the rock-n-roll bad-boy lifestyle to the very hilt. But when the girl of his dreams marries fellow rocker Brian Ellis, he buries his disappointment in the arms of an older woman. The following morning, Brett realizes what he experienced was only the beginning of a song he's been trying to write all his life. It's a seductive theme, which Tessa falls for again and again, but getting her to believe they have a hit is turning out to be far from a sure thing . . .

Chapter 1

Tessa walked outside, maintaining her happy expression past the knot of smokers by the door. This wedding shouldn't bug her so much. Brian had gotten over his crush on her years ago. Shit, he'd been married before. She'd fallen off his pedestal a long time ago. So why did this marriage seem like the end of the world?

Suzi made a beautiful bride. One of her friends had designed the simple white gown for her. Ribbons of rainbow colors started as faint pastels across the bust and gained intensity as they wrapped around her body and down the back of her dress until they formed a brilliant train. Daisies wound through her upswept hair and complemented her pretty, sweet face. Brian looked rather sharp, too, in his white tux, open at the throat. His best accessory, though, had to be the expression of utter joy in his eyes.

It made Tessa want to puke. Not because they were happy. No, never that. Brian deserved to be happy. Suzi did, too. Apparently, everyone deserved to be happy.

Except her.

"Nice show, huh?"

Tessa glanced at Brett who'd wandered up beside her at the overlook. Or maybe she'd wandered up beside him. The ocean smashed into the cliffs below as if it held a grudge against her. "Yeah. They look really happy."

"She's the Holy Grail," Brett said. He leaned on the guardrail, fiddling a cigarette between his fingers. "She was a total mess when she left Logan last year. I took her out to this place I go to. Never laid a hand on her."

Tessa nodded. Why did he think she should care? Everybody knew he'd pulled Suzi out of the party where she'd broken up with her last boyfriend, Logan, nearly a year ago. Tessa had been one of many people trying to figure out where the hell they'd gone for weeks before Suzi had reappeared at Jason's West Virginia place. "You're a big damn hero."

"Something like that." He flicked the cigarette off the cliff, unlit. "Brian's a good guy, right? He'll be good to her, won't he?"

"I've known him since he was a kid. He'd walk through hell for her." Brian was the best guy. Absolute heart of gold. If she'd been half awake ten years ago, she could have had that.

"Good. That's good. Cause next time I have to haul her away from some asshole, I'm not going to be so easygoing about letting her leave."

"What the fuck are you talking about?" She glared at Brett, but he looked like he'd been dragged backward through the desert by a tour bus, and she faltered. "What's wrong with you?"

Brett turned, stared at the ocean. "Probably the same thing that's wrong with you."

"What's that supposed to mean?"

"Oh, come on. How dumb do you think everybody is? You've known Brian since he was in elementary school. His daughter is named after you. The only person at this wedding who looks sicker about it is Logan." Brett bobbed his head. "And maybe me. You and Brian had a thing, or you wish you had a thing, or something. I'd say I could write a great song about it, but there's already been a bunch. Etta James did three or four."

"So, are you telling me that party-hearty Brett Cherney lost his poor little heart to the bride?" Tessa meant to smirk, but it came out twisted because of the sob she was trying to cover.

"Only as much as tough lawyer Tessa Callisto lost her heart to the groom."

Tessa stared back in the direction of the pavilion. Over six hundred guests. This wedding was almost as well attended as the Grammys. No point hiring a band because no local band could hold a candle to this audience, so music had been supplied by a running jam. Everyone was having a blast. They wouldn't notice a couple of people missing. "You know what the best cure for a broken heart is, don't you?"

"What?" He glanced over his shoulder as if the answer to her question was back at the wedding reception.

She stared into Brett's eyes. Brett, who slept with every female who caught his fancy. And there were lots of those. What with his lean build and washboard abs, he was such a very good-looking specimen. "Wanna?" She arched an eyebrow at him.

His lips curled into a smile. "Sounds good to me."

"Your place or mine?"

"I'm thinking of some place more neutral."

* * * *

Brett slammed her against the door as soon as it was closed. All the way here, she'd been teasing him. Running her hand up the inside of his thigh, dragging her fingers through his hair, toying with his earlobe. And every time he'd reached for her, she'd smacked his hand away and told him to watch the road.

"Your ass is mine now," he growled, pressing his face into the curve of her neck.

"I was hoping you wanted more than that."

"Believe me. I plan to have every inch of you before I'm done."

Laughing, she ripped his shirt open and shoved it down his arms. "Let's see if you can deliver on that promise."

"I can." He hiked up her skirt. "Pantyhose? Really? These fucking things are like a force field around your sweet spot."

"I was going to the wedding of an old and dear friend, not headed out for a sleazy tryst."

"Damn." Brett dropped to his knees and pulled at the pantyhose. Her heavy, lusty scent crawled through his brain and straight into his dick. "I didn't think women wore these things anymore."

"I'm not the kind of woman you usually undress."

"No kidding." He smoothed his hands down her soft thighs, down to— "Your fucking shoes have buckles on the ankles. Is there a lock on your pussy, too?"

She laughed again. He glanced up in time to see her toss her blouse across the room. Underneath, she'd worn a lacy bra. Hopefully, it had a normal clasp and not some exotic thing like her goddamn shoes. He fumbled with the buckle, but his fingers couldn't grasp it.

"Let me help you." She crouched, pinned between the door and him, trying to reach her shoes through the tangle of pantyhose. Her dark hair brushed his cheek, and he shivered. Tessa was hot. Way hotter than he'd ever thought.

"Screw that." Brett wrapped his arm around her waist and swung her onto the floor. "I can get to all the parts I need."

She buried her hands in his hair, drawing him into a deep kiss. Her tongue delved into his mouth as she ground her hips against his.

The urgent need in her touch sizzled along his skin. "You're a hell of a woman," he said, dragging his lips down her chest to the thankfully simple front clasp on her bra.

"Thanks, now quit wasting time."

"You on a schedule?" He flicked open the bra and curved his hand around the warm flesh of her breast.

"No, I just have a lot of work for you. You need to get busy."

"I love a take-charge woman." Reaching into his pocket, he located a condom.

"Then you are going to love me." She grabbed his pants and opened them. "You have a rubber? If not, I have some in my purse."

"I got it." He climbed to his knees and ripped open the foil. "Glad to know you have some, too. Wouldn't want to run out."

"I'm pretty sure the desk would send up more if we asked. I'm surprised they didn't give you a gift basket of them when we checked in." She stretched her arms over her head, which did delightful things to her shape.

"I don't bring women here." Brett lifted her nylon-bound ankles over his head and crawled between her legs.

"Except me." Tessa licked her lips. "And Suzi."

Her and Suzi. Brett closed his eyes as he thrust into her, trying to imagine Suzi under him and only feeling Tessa's hot, sleek body and wet, soft mouth. He wrapped his arms around her, riding her hard and fast, lost in the wild rhythm of their bodies sliding together. Her legs clenched around his hips as if she'd never let him go. Beneath him, her eyes were closed and her mouth open as she gasped. Her dusky skin was slick with sweat.

His control slipped, and he groaned. "I don't think I can wait."

"You'll make it up to me." She tightened her hold on him, arching her hips to meet his.

He came in a heated satin rush, his whole body aching in the crest. Throughout, he could feel her arms and legs around him. Cradling him. For once, he didn't feel like he was in free fall. Funny, but he didn't hate the sensation the way he'd always thought he would. It was safety. Security. It was... "Tessa," he murmured.

"Just finish the job." She dug her fingernails into his back.

He thrust against her again until she came apart in his arms.

Sighing, she let her head loll on the carpet. "That was distracting."

"No problem." Brett swallowed his disappointment. Distracting? He'd never been called that before. The women he'd had lately had been a little more impressed. Fame was very impressive to a groupie. But Tessa was no groupie. She'd been in the thick of fame when he was still singing in the school holiday pageant. "Glad I could be of help."

"I hope I was just as distracting for you." She ruffled her fingers through his hair.

"Definitely." Brett slithered down her body and between her legs. She sat up as soon as she could and went to work on her shoes as if he wasn't even in the room. Okay, weird. Though he wasn't sure why it was so important she pay attention to him. He'd gotten what he wanted. He should be happy she didn't want to cuddle. Standing, he pulled his pants up. "I guess I'll take a shower."

"Go ahead, but I'm just going to get you dirty again." She didn't look up from her shoes.

"Good. I'll get really clean so you have to work harder." He went into the bathroom and turned on the water. Then he leaned on the door and listened to her walk around the other room.

The famous Jason Callisto's sister and lawyer, Tessa, had always been unattainable. She not only outclassed him in fame, but in brains, and at the reception had appeared totally together until she'd walked away. That was the reason he'd followed her. Because she'd stopped looking cool and started looking more like he felt. Except that just now, she'd been utterly chill.

Brett ducked under the water. He should have known better than to think he knew her this quickly. They had one stupid thing in common. Being second best.

But Tessa was a pretty awesome second.

The bathroom door opened. Tessa peeked around the shower door. "Mind if I join you?"

Brett stepped back to give her room. "You got the shoes off."

"They aren't difficult. They just defeated you." Smirking, she draped her arms around his shoulders.

"Ha ha. I have some buckles that might defeat you." Brett let his hands slide down her sides with the flow of the water.

"I might let you try those out." She leaned on him, her skin velvet against his.

"I thought I'd distracted you enough."

"That was then. This is now."

"You're demanding."

"I think you can fulfill my demands." She picked up the soap and traced down his chest with it. "You were concerned about being dirty."

"You're not going to give me a chance to get clean, either." Brett studied her eyes, trying to figure out where she was going. Five minutes ago, she'd all but told him to get lost, and now, she was crawling all over him again.

"On the contrary, I'm going to clean you up." She rubbed the soap on a cloth and started sweeping the cloth across his chest. "How's that?"

"Nice."

"Take notes, because it's going to be your turn in a minute." The cloth dipped lower.

"I look forward to it." He did love a woman who knew what she wanted and wasn't afraid to spell it out.

"I'm sure you do," she purred. "You always were a show off."

"What do you know about me?"

"Everything I need to." She stroked with the cloth along his length, which was very interested in the stimulation.

"Everything you need to?"

"You're a sleazy little party boy riding on the success of his first little hit and sleeping with every willing female you can find."

"You have no respect for me at all, do you?"

"I have lots of respect for you." She shifted him into the water to rinse him off and handed him the washcloth. "Right now I need a little party boy to fuck me thoroughly, and you are just the one to do it." Her breathing was heavy and slow.

"Thanks." He ran the cloth between her full breasts. She looked great naked. How old was she anyway? Jason was about forty. She must be a couple years older than her brother. Had he been overlooking an entire group of hot women because none of the chicks he'd picked was over thirty?

"Think nothing of it."

He soaped around her ass. Bigger than most of his girls', but tight and toned. Tessa had some substance to her. He slid between her legs from behind, drawing her against him and getting a sweet moan out of her. Her mouth curved into a lush smile.

"I knew you'd be frisky enough." Then she pulled away and rinsed off. "I've never heard of this place. How did you find it?"

"One of the guys my mom went with brought her here."

"Oh?" Tessa lifted her hair and rolled her neck under the hot water. "She was a backup singer, wasn't she?"

"Yeah."

"OD'd about ten years ago?"

"How did you know?"

Opening her eyes, she turned off the water. "My job is to know things."

"About me?" Brett followed her out of the shower. He'd thought he went after her at the reception, but maybe it was the other way around. She was smart. Maybe she'd lured him outside.

"When you and Suzi took off together, Jason had me hunting you. Best place to start looking was your past. Your dad is a nice guy." She walked from the bathroom, still dripping.

"My dad?"

"I called him trying to find you. So how did you end up being the guy to rescue Suzi?" She shoved open the patio door and stepped outside.

"Right place, right time."

Tessa cocked an eyebrow at him. "And she just ran off with you."

"When we were on tour, I got to know her, and I happened to be right there when she needed to leave." Brett hoped the heat on his face was sun and not embarrassment.

"You wanted to get next to her."

"Fuck yes, I did." Blushing. Definitely. "With a nickname like Randy Mirandy and a hot bod like hers, who wouldn't?"

"Indeed." Tessa stepped into the infinity pool and settled where she could stare out over the desert.

Brett clambered into the water next to her. This place was his refuge. After he'd come here with Suzi, it had also been his place to regret. He'd spent hours soaking in this pool, wondering what kind of moron he'd been to let Suzi get away and if there had been anything he could have done to stop it. "What about you? You knew Brian since he was a kid. He was married before. Why's it a crisis now?"

Tessa lifted one leg, put it down, and lifted the other, pointing her toe at the sky before lowering it into the water. "Brian had a huge crush on me when he was a kid. Well, up until he was about twenty-two, but I wasn't interested."

"So now you want what some other chick has?"

"No," Tessa snapped, glaring at him. "It's just an ego blow that he's not going to be following me around anymore."

"Right. Because he was before."

"Fuck you."

"In a little bit. I'm comfortable now."

Tessa slouched in the corner. "I just can't believe all those guys got married like that. Bear and Maureen. Jason and Cassie. Marc and Alex. Now Brian and Suzi. Another one bites the dust. I've known all those guys since we were kids."

"Ty's not hitched up yet."

"He's probably meeting his one true love as we speak. I'll be running background checks on her tomorrow. My mother is dating a guy from Cassie's hometown. Connie's even dating."

"Who's Connie?"

"My sister."

"Everybody's married but you."

"I don't want to be married," she growled.

Brett held up his hands. "Hey, don't look at me. I'm not looking for a wife here, either." He eased into the water. "I love this place."

"It's nice. Very relaxing. What made you bring Suzi here?"

"I knew a shitload of people would be hunting for her, and she needed some time away. Nobody would look for her here."

"This where she had her miscarriage?"

"Yeah."

"That must have been rough."

"I took care of her." Brett shrugged. He'd stood outside the bathroom door, fretting about what to do. She hadn't wanted him to call a doctor, but she'd been in so much pain. And then she'd cried all night. Holding her and not being able to do a damn thing to help her had sucked, but it had been better than standing outside a door.

"She's one of those women who doesn't have babies easily. Brian's already got the two, so he doesn't care," Tessa said.

"Do we have to talk about Brian all the time?"

"I thought that's why we were here. Because we both came in second."

"Then maybe we should call Logan. He came in second, too."

Tessa shrugged. "Go ahead if you want to, but I'm over my orgy phase. You two have fun. You can sit around and talk about how perfect Suzi is."

"Suzi's really nice." Brett scowled. Suzi was nice. Really friendly and approachable. Every time she'd joined them on the road when his band was touring with her ex's band, she'd found time to sit and talk, even though Logan had wanted her chained to his wrist whenever he was offstage. Tessa could be as bitchy as she wanted, but she'd better not start talking shit about Suzi.

"I know. She's a great girl. Always has been. Did you know she tried to patch up Brian and Bonnie's marriage? I could have told her it was a waste of time."

Brett couldn't decide which was worse. Talking about Brian or talking about Suzi. "I'm hungry. I'm going to order some dinner. You want anything?"

Tessa frowned at the desert. "Rum and Coke. Steak, well done. Baked potato, butter, no sour cream. Steamed summer squash. And chocolate frosting."

"Frosting without the cake?"

She smiled at him. "It's for later."

Brett grinned back. At least if she was going to torture him by talking about Brian and Suzi, she would make up for it.

Meet the Author

Maggie Dallen is a huge fan of happily-ever-afters. She writes contemporary and YA romance and has been known to rewrite the endings to classic love stories to ensure that they end on a happy note. In Maggie's version, Ingrid Bergman does not get on the plane. She lives in Northern California and works at a yarn store to support her knitting addiction. For more info please visit maggiedallen.com.

Follow her on Twitter @Mag_Dallen.
Or connect with her on Facebook.